Firefly of Immortality

FIREFLY OF IMMORTALITY

THE GUARDIANS OF LIGHT SERIES

BOOK ONE

Kasey Hill

Azoth Khem Publishing
Huntsville, AL
April 2025

© Azoth Khem Publishing, 2025

ISBN: 978-1-945987-11-3
First Edition 2016
Second Edition 2019
Third Edition 2025

Azoth Khem Publishing
29931 Copperpenny Drive NW
Harvest, AL 35749
www.azothkhem.com

Ordering Information:
Quantity sales and exclusive discounts are available on quantity purchases by corporations, associations, and others. For details, contact the publisher at the address above. For orders by U.S. trade bookstores and wholesalers, please contact Azoth Khem Publishing: Tel: (256) 221-5498 or visit
www.azothkhem.com

Printed in the United States of America

Check out these other series by Kasey Hill

The Guardians of Light Series
Firefly of Immortality
The Shining Ones
Firefly: The Half-Blood Angel
The Valley of the Shadow of Death: Nephilim Rising

Dark Woods Series
Devil's Claw

The Whispering Spirits Series
The Haunting at Foxwood Village
Dark Coven

Coming Soon to The Guardians of Light Series
Firefly of Immortality II
Black Wings of Death
Firefly of Immortality: Anniel Unveiled
Alpha and Omega
Firefly of the Apocalypse

Coming Soon to The Guardians of Light Series Universe

The Guardians of Light: Darkness Falls Series
Bloodlines: Into the Shadows

For my Luxina, the starchild

Firefly of Immortality

CHAPTER 1

*I*n the beginning

"THE SEAS WILL RISE and crash anew, spreading the waters of the vast deep blue. My arms in yours and your lips to mine, forever our souls to be intertwined. My light is yours as your grace is mine, together our powers are combined. But come morning as the dawn will approach, your hand will falter and let go. You take the dive, selfless and out of control. Just so in the end you may save their souls."

THERE HAS ALWAYS BEEN a war between the angels. It was not over who was heavenly and who was hellish, but rather over existing in heaven, to begin with. That war continues in an eternal battle of bloodshed while the brotherhood shared between them collapses. The Holy War was declared to the countless people of the earth throughout time, leaving them starved of knowledge, and empty of understanding, as to what exactly this war was about. Humanity was deceived into believing that the ultimate power named "God" was a creator of good, and his Adversary, Satan, was evil. The age-long battle of "good" versus "evil" at the tip of everyone's consciousness, yet it was never elaborated upon.

A space unoccupied in the vast array of the cosmos was claimed by a youthful god who called himself Alpha. When he leapt into being, he knew naught of the laws of the universe. He contemplated long and hard about what he would create from this void of space. It was full of darkness and hopelessness.

He had existed in solitude for eons before deciding that he no longer wished to be alone. Therefore, gathering the energy that surrounded him and existed within himself, he created another power to share in his experience; he called her Omega. Never had he imagined that he would create such a gem that enraptured his heart. Pure love streamed between the two of them, and together, they emanated so much love that they shared their plentiful love with the cosmos, causing galaxies to spring forth in the vast spaces of the universe. Their love produced so much power; inadvertently, they generated celestial creatures most like themselves. These beings were called angels and would be forever immortalized as the Elohim, both a cosmic and celestial hierarchy.

When they created this race of angels, their purpose was to be watchers and guardians of the universe. The cosmos was still empty of mortal men, but they wanted everyone to know their duties, and they wanted them to know that humanity, when created, was to be loved as much as their mother and father, if not more.

"You do understand the power and obedience you grant and receive by agreeing to this, do you not?" Omega asked. The angels nodded their heads in approval of their tasks. Disobedience to their mother and father was not a thing they wished to accomplish.

Once all the Elohim had agreed to love and trust the mortals, Omega, the goddess, waved her hand, and a desolate planet that had been molten lava had water crash through it. The raging fire and lava became landmasses, and the water filled in the rest, creating lakes, rivers, and oceans. They placed all sorts of creatures upon the land to roam and create

3

life from the life they were granted. They knew it would take quite some time for these creatures to go through their evolutionary trials, but Alpha and Omega could not wait for these creatures to evolve, so, they created a place outside of space and time that they called the Garden of Eden. They created morning and night for their precious treasures, and every angel gathered around so they could watch these creatures live.

They had yet to put any humans in the Garden, so they spent their time adding animals that they felt deserved to exist forever. Likewise, they placed many species of plant life that would never take root in Earth's soil. It was many years before Alpha and Omega decided it was time to create any humans for the Garden. When the time came, they created one human to exist in the Garden, and they called him Adam. Showering Adam with love and affection, he had everything he would ever need to survive in this Garden. Alpha and Omega were pleased with what their shared power had created. It was beautiful.

However, what brightens the heart and soul does not always last forever. Alpha noticed that there was an unequal balance in the cosmos. There was too much light and not enough darkness to keep the energies in balance. It was a perfect balance of yin and yang energies with just Omega and Himself, but with the addition of their celestial children, the universe was becoming more complicated.

Without Omega's knowledge or the Elohim's, Alpha sought council from beings that had secretly brought him into existence. Alpha was a jealous god at heart, and he knew that if they were to find out about others like him in power, they would turn their backs on him and leave. He traveled across galaxies and into different universes to pull council with the Elder Gods.

"I stand before you as a young god, but no less powerful than any of you. However, my universe is beginning to fold in upon itself, and I haven't the slightest idea as to why. I created for myself a consort, and we then created our own band of cosmic power through our children. Is this addition of power to the light the cause of my troubles? Tell me, what must I do to rectify this flaw in our universe?" Alpha looked into the eyes of the wisest of gods, hoping for rectification.

"You stand before me claiming yourself as powerful as I and yet have no clue as to how to fix your problem. Arrogance will get you nowhere, Alpha," the mighty god Drac thundered.

"Have I not created a universe full of spectrum as you have? Have I not gathered the energy within me to create for myself a mate as godly as yours?" Alpha replied bitterly.

"Even with these accomplishments, you still have no clue as to how to truly rule your universe — you fool. Instead of creating life, you created power. Instead of creating your world, you created an army to bow to you, and then ask why your universe caves in on itself. Such naivety from a boastful young god," Drac sneered.

"Please, I implore you. How do I rectify this situation?" Alpha pleaded, looking between the council faces.

"What was the first thing you did to this universe you created?" A voice called out; Alpha turned his gaze to a stunning goddess that held placement in the council.

"I created light where there was no light," Alpha replied indignantly. The goddess snickered. "Why do you mock me with my decisions of how my universe was brought about? Who do you think you are to condescend me in this tumultuous gift I gave this universe."

"I am the one who created the darkness. I am, in fact, darkness itself. Have you not heard of your Elder God, Tiamat?" she replied sarcastically.

Alpha became nervous as he glanced around to all the benevolent faces. "Apologies, Dark One," he said, taking to his knee in respect. He glanced up at her nervously for fear she may strike him down with her wrath. "How do I fix this chaos I have implemented upon myself?"

The insidious smile she gave him chilled him to his

core. "There is but one solution to the universe you have created for yourself. Since so much power exists in the light and is throwing the cosmos into discord, you must choose an adversary to oppose you."

"What do you mean, an adversary?" Alpha, confused by her instructions, rose to his feet and approached the council.

"The natural order and balance of the cosmos are out of sorts. An adversary would balance the energies of your universe, your energies being that of light, and your Adversary being that of darkness. Do not confuse the two as negative oppositions but as positives. The dark and light are drawn to one another and complete a cycle of energy. Right now, the energy of the universe is one-sided and is the root cause for the disruption of your universe." The council all nodded in agreement with Tiamat.

"I still do not quite understand what you mean for me to do," Alpha replied.

"One of your creations must adhere to the darkness and be your counter energy," Tiamat replied. "And you call yourself all-knowing." She chuckled while she toyed with him.

"I must sacrifice one of my own to bring about the balance of the energies," Alpha stated, letting the information sink in. Tiamat nodded. "Does it matter who?" he asked.

"It must be one whose power is in close proximity to your own," she replied.

Alpha sighed heavily as he drank in everything she had told him. "I thank you all for joining council with me. I now know my answer and must implement it immediately." The council nodded their approval of his disclosing statement and faded back to the universes they held power over. Alpha returned to the summit and was greeted by Omega at the gates.

"I was wondering where you were." She smiled at him and wrapped her arms around his neck, kissing him softly on the lips.

"I wasn't far," he replied. "Gather the children, darling. We need to sit down and have a talk with them." Omega wrinkled her forehead in confusion but nodded, acknowledging she would. She assembled the court with a mandatory proclamation that all angels must be present.

CHAPTER 2

*T*o Have Loved and Lost

"YOU LEFT me without letting me know why? Why!!? I demand to know why! But your answer still falls on my deaf ears. I walk from your feet to the reflecting light bouncing in my eyes I walk closer to your heart. And I lay down your flowers right there on the mound of dirt."

I WALKED to the center of the graveyard, maneuvering the way I had remembered it. It had been four years since the day Gramms had died. It still stings as if it were only yesterday. I swear, if I didn't know any better, someone took my emotions after my breakdown, and they were slowly giving them back to me. *Ridiculous right?* I decided to go to her grave for the first time since we had buried her. Everyone thought it would have been best not to visit until the wound had scabbed over. *Could it ever really scab over?*

I sat down at her feet and laid the peonies I bought for her at her headstone. Peonies were always her favorite. I slipped the Bible she had read to me every night that she was over at my house out of my bag. I flipped the pages open and ran my fingers over them. The night Gramms died, she had come over like she had done weekly ever since my young mind could remember. That night seemed no different from any other night. Gramms would come over to cook me dinner while my parents locked themselves away in their room, arguing. We had already sat down and had the big "D" discussion, but they promised to work it out beforehand. Their arguments had started to become rapid in frequency, so I knew the time would be soon.

"What are you cooking tonight, Gramms," I asked, walking into the kitchen.

"Well, do you still like spaghetti?" she asked, winking at me.

"Oh, how did you know it is my favorite?" I asked, chuckling.

I walked over to the stove and lifted the lid off the pot, bubbling with pasta sauce. The aroma filled my nostrils, and my stomach growled in response. Gramms chuckled back at me and cooed, "Tell it not to worry. Dinner's nearly ready." I smiled at her humor and sat down at the table.

Gramms' Bible was laid out and opened midways through to some strange writing. She had to have taken foreign language classes in ancient writings. You could hardly call the scribbles words. "Are you going to read to me again tonight?" I asked, looking up from her book.

"Don't I always?" she replied.

"Mom doesn't like it when you read to me from it. She said you're filtering into my mind nothing but pure nonsense," I said. "Well, that wasn't the exact word she used, but I'd rather not pick up her bad habit of cursing," I added.

Gramms busied herself, making our plates of spaghetti and removed the French bread from the oven. She cut us slices from the loaf of baked bread, served me my plate, and took a seat across from me. We ate in silence for a few moments. Mom's comments always made her upset whenever she spoke out against the family bible.

"Sophie, do you go to church with your mother still?" she asked.

"Yup, Mom said I have to, so I wouldn't be sucked into the evilness of the world," I replied.

"The evil of the world indeed," Gramms said angrily. "Do you know what church really promotes?" she asked coolly. I shook my head. "Throughout time, the church has used this propaganda to fund their war on 'Satan.' Donations and 'offerings' have poured in from billions of churchgoers to pay for new churches to be built to pay the salary of preachers, priests, and even the Pope. Fear and torment have spread worldwide, accusing those who do not bow to the church and its teachings of being a follower of Satan. Hell was the destination of those who did not convert, and death was implemented in the early start of Christianity. The brush upon the blade and cross spread throughout the Middle East and into the European nations. Blood was shed in this "holy" war, and it wasn't the blood of soldiers, but rather the blood of innocence. Your mother is just sucking you into THAT nonsense." She was building in anger.

"What else has the church lied about, Gramms?" I asked, taking slow bites from my food.

"Satan became a front for the church, a way to convert those who were already afraid of dying for not wanting to convert. The image of the goat-like beast papered the painted glass of the Roman Catholic Church and was a warning to those who did not follow word by word the holy text taught that they would end up a slave to him. Demons came next, the minions of Satan. They were angels who chose to fall with him instead of staying with their father in heaven. Thus began the holy war not only on Earth but also in between Heaven and Purgatory. What the church left out, not by choice, but by the influence of 'God' himself, was that the war was instigated by God, not by those who had fallen." She was waving her hands around in the air as she made her points.

I grew quiet and finished eating my food. Overhead, I heard the thuds and thumps coming from my parent's room. I excused myself from the table, muttering that I needed to use the restroom, and inched closer to their door to hear what they were arguing about this time.

"She's fourteen, Lorraine. Your mother needs to stop telling her about her Satanic beliefs before she converts our daughter into a Satanist!" Dad shouted.

"My mother is not a Satanist! She just has a separate set of beliefs than what mainstream religion has," my mother retorted bitterly.

"Well, tonight is the last night. If you want this marriage to work, you're going to have to put your foot down and tell her enough is enough!" I heard their master bathroom door slam shut, and it startled me.

I couldn't believe Dad would say that about Gramms. I slipped back downstairs, and Gramms had already washed the plates we ate from and slipped into the living room. I tried to hold back the tears wanting to roll down my face. Gramms patted the seat beside her, so I walked over to her and curled up beside her.

"I'm sorry you had to hear that, Sophie. Your parents are lashing out at anything they can to fuel their arguments." She smoothed my hair out while she talked to me. "Your hair has always been my envy, your red, bouncy curls. Let me braid it," she said.

I climbed to the floor in front of me, and she ran a brush through my hair. "Did you know that left unknown throughout time, there was a family lineage that started in the early days after the banishment from the Garden?" she asked.

"You mean like the stories you told me as a kid?" I asked.

"Exactly like those stories," she said. "Guardians were created, as an opposition of God, to thwart the war. The lineage held a secret and passed the secret on through a family bible. This Bible told the true story of what happened, and every so often, one was born into the family to help diminish the ideologies that the Father God implemented. It was up to this person to determine what was truth and what was false. This lineage had made it through all the millenniums of war and anguish both sides fought for."

"Well, where is the lineage at now?" I asked.

"We're that lineage, Sophie," she replied.

"You mean your bible is the same bible?"

"Yes, it is," she replied. "Sweetie, it is particularly important that you understand the story of creation. As Guardians, it is vital to our nature that we understand our responsibility from this story. No one knew exactly where the lineage started or when it would end, but it was always up to the chosen person in the family to uphold the beliefs."

Her stories and beliefs came from legends of a fall, not that of Satan, but of the Dark Mother. I knew everyone had heard some form of the creation story. God created Adam and Eve; they sinned and were forced from the Garden of Eden. They were no longer pure, so they could no longer see the Garden, making it lost to civilization. *Right?* Well, not according to the book passed down through Gramms' family. Every religion has its own perception that was passed down by word of mouth through angels and even God himself. Gramms' Bible claimed to know the real story behind it all.

"Why does it have my name in the book, Gramms?" I asked.

"If it was your responsibility to guard the secret of

15

the Garden, would you give it to the Angel, to the Fallen, or keep it to yourself?" she asked.

"I wouldn't give it to the fallen angels. They are demons, Gramms," I replied.

"They are not demons," she said irritated. "Have you not paid any attention to the stories I tell you?"

I felt bad for saying it, but if it kept my parents together, then I wouldn't stray into the stories she told. "Yes, but it's just a book, Gramms. There's no evidence, no proof. It's time for me to grow up and realize that it's all just a story that never happened. There was one God that created everything, and his Adversary is the Devil, not the Dark Mother."

"Well, you have four more years to decide," she replied, finishing the bow in my hair.

"What happens in four years, Gramms?" I asked.

I waited for her to answer. She had never mentioned anything special would happen on my eighteenth birthday. I felt a chill in the air, and the hairs on my neck pricked up. She had grown completely silent and still.

"Gramms?" I asked, looking over my shoulder at her. She was slumped in the chair, barely breathing. "Gramms! Mom!" I started to run off, but she grabbed me by my arm.

"Listen to me, Sophie, your decision affects the entire world and balance of things." Tears streamed down my face as she clutched her chest.

"Mom! Dad! Help!" I screamed, trying to wrench from her grasp to call an ambulance.

"Do not let your mother or father cloud out your own judgment. Believe....oh...what you want... to believe." Her arm let go of mine and fell to the side of the chair as her last breath escaped her lips. "MOM!!!!!" I screamed at the top of my lungs.

They came bounding down the stairs, and I stood there, shaking Gramms, trying to get her to respond to me. Dad pushed me out of the way and lay her down on the floor to start CPR. Mom picked up the phone and called for help.

"This is your fault!" I screamed out. My parents looked over at me. "All she wanted was for someone to listen to her, to believe in what she said. All you two cared about was saving your marriage! She heard you just as I did!"

"Sophie," Dad called out. I started for the door when Mom grabbed my arm. I wrenched loose from her and ran out the door.

I sat out on the front porch crying. The rest of the night happened in a blur. I remember the ambulance coming, taking her away, and then leaving. I disappeared from the house and ran through the various parts of the neighborhood. Every blind turn I took brought me back to the house when all I wanted to do was get away. I was eventually picked up by the police and brought back home.

I remember a calm feeling descending over me,

making me immediately comforted, but no clue as to why or what it was. As I drifted off to sleep, I heard voices that weren't my mom or my dad speaking.

"Do you think Michael or Uriel did it?" a manly voice asked.

"I'm not sure. What I do know is that she wasn't supposed to pass until the day before her 18th birthday," a woman replied. *How could these people know when she was supposed to die?* "We need to report this matter as soon as possible," she said.

"Agreed, it looks as if they are playing dirty when it clearly breaks the law. I was sure they found a loophole somewhere, and yet, they're supposed to be the 'good guys.' Humph!" the man's voice replied.

"Shh, not so loud she is stirring awake," the woman hissed.

I felt another wave of a lulling lullaby without words. I caught a glimpse of a shadow in the corner of my room, but I was overwhelmed by exhaustion and fell into a deep sleep.

I sat there, thinking everything over at her grave. Even the days leading up to her funeral felt odd to me. The days went by fast and numb. I couldn't even feel anything to cry. I felt completely deprived of emotions, just as I had felt lulled to sleep that night. There was a large turnout of people who showed up for the wake and funeral. Some I knew, some I had never laid eyes on before. There were some kids from school that came to lend me their condolences. I murmured my thanks to them as they came up and gave their hugs. The only person who didn't move from his spot was Isaiah. He just sat at the back of the room and watched me. Pain was etched on his face. A few of his friends made whispering comments in his ear, but he didn't budge.

He was always quiet, even in school. Hardly a word was spoken to anyone, and it seemed as if the teachers always skipped him for answering questions. We grew up together on the same street, so I have known him since childhood. Gramms took him and a few other kids in when they were younger and orphaned. I didn't know where they would go now. I hoped they wouldn't be relocated to a different town. We were always friends, always close, that is until my mother started taking me to church. He completely changed after that. I once confronted him on the issue. I was hurt and alone in the world without my friend. I asked him if he was Jewish, Islamic, or anything as to why it offended him that I began going to church. He never replied.

I realized the entire time I had been zoning and staring at him, he had returned my gaze and watched me. It was normal for me to zone out during times when I needed comfort. For a split second, I looked away from him. When I returned my look, he was gone. I looked around the room frantically, but he wasn't anywhere to be seen. It was then that everything sank in. I felt utterly alone, and all the emotions I had been holding back came boiling to the surface.

I was told later that I had a nervous breakdown. It was just a week or two until school was to start back up, and honestly, I had lost all sense of time. I couldn't even tell you the dates if they weren't etched on her grave. Of course, I was treated with exceptional care, and even to this day, I still am. Most people are afraid to bring up what happened for fear that it will cause me to lose it again. I felt like an outcast and still do.

"I know it sounds silly. I know you really read to me from this book. I read it myself, too, while you were alive. I... I don't understand why I can't see what you read to me or even the first page with the poem on it." A tear slid down my cheek as I talked to her. "It's the only thing I have of you, and I can't even read the amazing stories you told me from it. I can only live in the memory of what we shared. The pages are all blank or in a language I can't understand." I sniffed, wiping away another tear. "Gramms, I miss you so much!" There it was, the waterfall release I so desperately needed. I lay on her grave and cried. I was there for hours. The sun went from high in the sky to barely peeking over the horizon, but I didn't care. It was something I had to do. I could've sworn I fell asleep on the grave. I didn't remember walking home, but I ended up back at home, in my bed, waking to the sunrise.

My head throbbed from where I had cried so much at her grave. I went and hopped in the shower. I made sure my blotchy and puffy face was covered with makeup before I made a grand appearance in front of my mom. I walked over to the counter in the kitchen and pulled a mug from the cabinet. I then walked to the coffee pot and poured a steaming, fresh cup of coffee. I sniffed the aroma, and it began to ease the tension in my head and neck.

"How did yesterday go?" my mom asked as she walked in the kitchen behind me, scaring the crap out of me. I jumped, nearly spilling the coffee everywhere. I walked over to the table and sat down.

"It was fine. Something I needed to do," I responded, sipping on the coffee and reading the paperback I left on the kitchen table for my morning read.

"I know it always bothered you that she passed just a few days before your birthday. You were such a strong young woman burying your grandmother on your birthday." She thought she was comforting me, but she wasn't. She was making everything worse again. After Gramms died, Dad left. He couldn't take the emotions in the house anymore. I get a birthday card every year, but he never comes to see me. Mom said he remarried and has a new family now. I can't see how he could abandon eighteen

21

years' worth of love with his child for a new family. It is what it is, I guess.

"It's fine, Mom," I said, dropping my book and downing what was left of my coffee. "Gotta split. I start my job today, and I don't want to be late." I bent down, kissed her cheek, and was out the door before she could protest. My job didn't start for another five hours, but I couldn't sit and listen to her anymore. Just as I was opening the door to my car, she popped her head out of the house.

"Tonight, the church is having a late-night sermon in honor of your grandmother. Do you want to go?" she asked with a hopeful smile. She knew my answer before it even left my lips. I quit church the same night Gramms died. Most people said they saw the light within me die the day she did; a lot of people said I changed when she died. I didn't know, but I wasn't going to disappoint her and let them brainwash me with whatever stories their Bible told.

"I won't be off work in time, sorry. Maybe next time?" I asked as I plopped in my car seat.

She frowned, went back inside, and shut the door behind her. Gramms' Bible tugged at my mind. I dug it out of the bag I snatched from the chair in the kitchen before I escaped to my car. I ran my fingers along the cover of it. The book always brought back memories of her. It smelled old, the pages looked ancient, and the cover was leather-bound. It had a magnificent tree etched into the leather.

I just wished I could read the stories she used to tell me. As I put the book back in my bag, something smacked my driver's window, scaring me. I screamed like a little kid and then heard laughing. I looked over and saw Dean standing there. He had a devilish look in his eye and a crooked grin.

I rolled my window down in annoyance. "You scared me!" I yelled at him.

"Sorry, I thought you were getting ready to pull out. I was wondering if I could catch a ride with you into town."

His eyes glinted in the sun. They were so the most amazing shade of blue-gray. No, I take that back. Blue-gray doesn't even compare to the color they were. It was as if you were staring into the sky itself during the day with the glow of the moon in them. He was new to town and had just moved in up the street a few days ago.

"Do you want to be shown around or just dropped off?" I asked.

"Just dropped off. I met a few guys yesterday and seemed to hit it off with them, so they invited me out to play football with them." I motioned for him to get into the car. He walked to the passenger side and climbed in. I watched as the curtain in the living room dropped, as my nosy mom was probably doing cartwheels over the boy talking to me. I wasn't much into having boyfriends. Don't get me wrong. I looked, but I had so much on my plate that I couldn't tolerate a boyfriend. It would only be a matter of time before he found out how screwed up my life was, and he wouldn't be interested in me anymore.

"Just let me know where to drop you off, and I will," I said, giving a faint smile.

He grinned back at me. There was something that twinkled in his eye that I couldn't quite grasp.

"So, I'm sorry, what's your name again? I'm horrible with names. My mom is always saying I need to have a memory card installed into my brain," he chuckled.

I pretended to smile at the joke, although it wasn't that funny. "I'm Sophie."

"Ah, that's right. I remember now. Making a mental note of it now," he said, putting his finger to his temple.

He grinned, and I half grinned back. He rolled his window down, and the most heavenly aroma filled the car. It was hypnotic and dizzying.

"Is that your cologne I smell? It's...like heaven in a bottle!" I said, breathing in another breath. He stiffened and rolled his window back up. "Was that a hint of lavender and myrrh?" I asked, looking over at him.

"No, it must have been the wind you smelled. I'm not wearing cologne." We were just passing by the recreational center when he told me to pull off there.

I saw the boys from school all running around in the field, chasing one another. "You should sit and watch us play," he said, smiling at me.

I nearly choked on my laugh. I was not the kind of girl that sat around watching boys play games.

"It'll be fun," he said, his eyes glinting at me. *Was he seriously flirting with me?* I felt my cheeks flush a bit.

I didn't know why, but I agreed. "But," I started adding to the compromise, "my job starts in a few hours, so I can't stay all day," I said as I made my way out of the car and over to his side.

He grabbed my hand up, and I felt the blood rush to my face and through my body. No one has ever held my hand or shown me this amount of attention before. We walked to the field together, and I could feel eyes everywhere on me. The girls sitting there were watching me in amazement, envy, and hatred. Their eyes burned into my skin. It's not my fault that he's my next-door neighbor, and it wasn't like I was staking a claim on him. I only offered him a ride, but none of this, I said out loud. My eyes flitted back over to the field of boys. Some of them watched him walk with me to the bleachers and kiss my hand as he made his way out to the group. I recognized half of the boys. The other half must be from one town over. One surprise I didn't expect to see was Isaiah among the group of boys. He looked ready to pounce on Dean as he walked over to the group of boys. His eyes danced from Dean to me, and he glared a look at Dean that I had never seen him ever make before. His face darkened, and I could see his fists tighten.

All the boys on the field stood in between Dean and Isaiah. Dean's back was to me, so I couldn't even see what kind of look he had been giving Isaiah back. Someone patted Isaiah's back, and he let go of his stance. It was almost as if they all had conversations in their heads because not a word was uttered. As soon as his body tension dropped, the overcast sky disappeared. *Weird, I hadn't even noticed it cloud up.* I watched him throw his hands up, mumbling something as he stalked off the field. He walked right by me and looked at me. I could see in his eyes he desperately wanted to tell me something. Instead, he turned around and continued walking toward where all the cars were parked.

I wasn't letting him get off the hook that easy. I ran after him as he walked down the road.

"Isaiah!" I yelled.

He stopped in his tracks but didn't turn around.

"What is going on? Were you mad I showed up with Dean?"

I could've sworn I saw him flinch.

"Why don't you ever talk to me? I show up at the field with my new next-door neighbor, and you're ready to beat him to a pulp. Yet, you won't even talk to me."

He stood there with his back turned. I could tell he was breathing hard.

"Please, talk to me. You shut me out completely years ago, and I don't know why! Please, just let me back in. I miss being friends."

I expected him to turn around, run, and kiss me or something.

Instead, he said, "Go home, Sophie. It's not safe for you to be here." He then began walking to his house without another word uttered.

I looked over to the group of boys who were playing ball, and they had all stopped to watch what we had to say to one another. I swear I could see Dean smirking. The rest of their faces were blank and unreadable. I walked back to my car and was about to open the door when Dean appeared out of nowhere, standing there.

"You're not going to let that punk ruin your fun, are you?" he asked, smiling a lopsided grin. He picked my hand up again, but this time I shook it free from his grip.

"I happen to know that 'punk' a lot better than I do you, and if he doesn't think I should hang around you, most of the time, he is right," I retorted back. I climbed into my car and started the engine when he leaned in my window.

"You are making a terrible decision."

He had no smile this time but an ice-cold look that chilled me to the bone. I saw a few of the other boys I knew make their way for my car when he bolted to the other side of the road. A car pulled up. He jumped in and took off with them. *He was so weird!* The boys made it to my car just as the other car Dean jumped in peeled away.

"You okay, Sophie?" Rafe asked as he leaned in my window.

Rafe was another of the foster children Gramms had taken in. He went by Rafe since his name, Raphael, was so outdated. I was a bit shocked, but I was okay. There was just something about his eyes that made me cringe.

"I'm fine, Rafe," I replied, shaking off the uneasy feeling I had.

"Are you sure?" he pushed a little harder.

I smiled, "I'm fine. Don't worry about me."

His eyes didn't release their tense gaze, but he did look away down the road in the direction both the car and Isaiah had gone. As if some invisible command had been called, the boys pulled up beside him in Sam's Jeep, and Rafe jumped in. They tore off down the road in the direction everyone went.

I didn't know why, but curiosity got the best of me. So, instead of heading into town as planned, I followed everyone else. I didn't know how I knew exactly which way they had gone, but I ended up at the same place they did. I parked my car a block up the street and walked down to where I could hear them speak. It was a public playground, but there weren't any children to be seen.

"You're to stay away from her," Isaiah yelled with a tone I had never heard from him. It was dark and angry.

"You know the rules. This is the year, and she is the One." Dean smirked at Isaiah. *The One? The one what?*

"You will not touch her or get near her again!" Isaiah yelled, and thunder clapped.

Odd, that was another weather anomaly that appeared during his anger.

"We can settle this the easy way, or we can settle this the hard way. I'm sure Father will be displeased if we choose the hard way," Dean sneered, sarcasm dripping from the bite.

"He is NOT my father!" Isaiah yelled back at Dean.

Dean just laughed at him.

"Say what you will, do what you may. This is the year, and she is the One. Before she turns nineteen, she will disclose to me what we all have wanted to know for years! The Garden will be ours again soon, Brother. Father has already won one battle, and Mother is no longer remembered. It won't be long until Sophie is the same way!" Dean chided.

Isaiah snapped and charged at Dean. Sam and Rafe jumped in front of him and held him back. I watched as Azazel, Sam's sister, climbed from the Jeep and walked over to the boys squaring off.

"Enough! All you! You stupid asses just busted yourselves out. She heard everything!"

Oh no! She knew I was here. I didn't know why, but I turned and ran from the spot I was standing in back to my car. No sooner had I reached the door handle than someone grabbed me from behind. I prayed in my head that it wasn't Dean who grabbed me, and I heard a chuckle from the one who grabbed me. I was still being held from behind as the vehicle that Dean was in drove by with his face glaring at the group, and then he looked at me with a sly grin. Once the vehicle was out of sight, I figured the arms around me would drop their hold on me, but they did not.

"I told you to go home, Sophie." Of course, it was Isaiah holding me in place. Even though I figured it would be a rough grab, he held me gently. His arms held me by my waist, and I loved the feeling. Warmth crashed through me, and I could feel my cheeks superheated.

"What- what were y'all talking about? What did he mean by 'me'?" I asked.

I heard him sigh, and I looked around at the group that surrounded me, all their eyes looking from me to him.

"Well, are we going to tell her?" Azazel asked. I felt him tense up as she stared at him.

"It's not her birthday yet. You know the rules," he hissed.

"Well, the rules have already been broken by them! We must inform her about what's going on!" Sam yelled.

He sighed again. "Can I tell her alone?"

"However, it is told, whenever it is told, whoever tells her, it needs to be done before he sinks his claws back into her," Rafe said. "Let him tell her by himself. It might be better coming from just him than all of us and everything at once."

"Tell me what? What are y'all talking about?" I was becoming impatient and very quickly.

"Sophie, do you have your grandmother's Bible?" Isaiah asked.

"How... how do you know about that?" I asked, confused.

I didn't remember him ever being over while she had read from the book to me. I doubt she would have read it to them since it was a treasured family heirloom, and they were just foster kids.

"I will explain as we drive to her grave," he said as he let my waist go and climbed in the driver seat. I stood there, dumbfounded. "Get in."

I walked to the passenger side door and looked at everyone else. They all looked serious, so I knew it had to be serious and not some sort of game. I climbed in, and Isaiah put the car in drive. We started for the cemetery while the car remained void of sound.

"I wish you had gone home as I asked you to," he

said, breaking the silence. "I figured this one request of you after years of silent stares that you would have at least listened to me."

"You make it seem like I was the one ignoring you! You were the one who quit being my friend and at the right time, too, the time when I needed you the most, the year she died! I had no one to talk to." I blurted it out without even thinking. My cheeks immediately flushed, and I could tell he sensed my embarrassment.

"I had to quit talking to you. It was against the rules for me to have gotten as close to you as I did. I was already chastised by Sam for it." I could tell he wasn't supposed to have said that either.

"Who is Sam to tell you who you can and can't get close to," I retorted back.

"Please, Sophie, just let me get to the cemetery, and I will tell you everything. I promise. If we go in order, it will be better than hodge-podging all over the place with facts." He didn't say anything else, and the look on his face said he wasn't going to. I didn't push it from him.

Oh, my God! Work! "Ughhh!" I groaned.

"What? What is it?" he asked in sincere worry.

"I start a new job today, and I'm late. Great impression for the first day, right? Idiot!" I facepalmed myself.

"I already took care of that," Isaiah said, smirking.

"Huh? How?"

"I knew you weren't going to listen, and what was going to happen. I called in for you while walking down the road. The town knows what today is; you start tomorrow." I stared at him in disbelief.

"How did you 'know' I wasn't going to listen, or for that matter, what was going to happen?" I asked in a whisper.

"You never do." He grinned at me, and I socked him in the arm. He laughed. It was so wonderful to hear his laugh and to hear his voice again.

"I've missed you." It slipped out.

I'm such a moron. It's barely been half a day, just a small conversation, and I was already pouring my heart out to him. I knew my cheeks reddened once more. I heard him sigh. Whatever he wanted to say back to me, he withheld. We pulled into the cemetery, and he drove over to where my grandmother's grave was nestled.

"How do you remember where it is?" I asked, unbuckling my seatbelt.

He didn't respond and got out of the car.

"Don't forget the book," he said.

I fished the book from my bag and followed him over to Gramms' grave.

"Normally, this is mother to daughter, but your mother has chosen the other side as opposed to our side."

He took the book from my hands and threw up

33

his finger as I was about to ask him what he meant.

"Mariam, please assist me."

He was nuts! I hadn't realized how Gramms' death affected him. I was about to interject when swirling blue lights gathered all around me. I began to retreat, but he grabbed my hand and held it. The touch was magnetic and sent a shock through me, but he didn't drop my hand. The blue lights formed into a body, and then Gramms' face appeared.

"If you think this is some sort of joke, it's not funny!" I was pissed, beyond pissed, actually.

"Sophie, listen to him when he talks to you. Nice to see you, Incaendiel." *What? His name is Isaiah, not Inca- whatever she said.*

"You have to be quick, Mariam. They have already sent the snake down to start in on her, the same one as last time. We must not lose her to the other side!" His eyes pleaded with Mariam's.

"Sophie, do you remember the stories I used to read to you from the book?" I stared in disbelief. *This had to be my Gramms.* All I could do was nod. "Do you have the book?" Isaiah laid it on the ground in front of her. "Pick the book up, Sophie, and open it to the first page."

"It's blank. There's nothing in it," I said, picking the book up.

"Just open it, my dear." I obeyed and opened it to the first page.

The page was blank at first, but then letters began to swirl around and appear. I stared in disbelief as they manifested throughout the entire book.

"Remember the last time I was reading to you from the book, and I told you it was important for you to remember the book? Well, this is the reason why. The heavens are at war with their fallen brothers. The creation story and everything I told you from the book is true. Remember the guardians that hold the secret to the Garden of Eden?" I nodded my head. "Well, they are here for the location. Every one thousand years, they come to us searching for it, and the last time nearly got it. So, I assume that is why they sent the same angel back for it once more since you nearly gave in last time."

"What? I wasn't born one thousand years ago. I'm only 17."

"You are a reincarnated soul, my Sophie. Only you possess the knowledge as to where the Garden of Eden exists. Also, you are the key to the Gates of the summit."

I was speechless.

"They thought by ending my life earlier than what it was supposed to have been that they would have had the upper hand."

"Wait, angels killed you?" I was stunned. I looked at Isaiah. "And you...you're a demon?"

He tensed up and glared at me. "We are NOT demons! We are Wanderers, those who chose to fall, but because he requested it!" I made him mad. I had hit a nerve and was really wishing I hadn't.

"So, you're not even human. All this time...you lied to me about who you are! Your name isn't even Isaiah. It's Inca- whatever she called you, but yet, I'm supposed to believe the ones who lied to me over the ones who haven't even tried to sweet-talk their way into my life."

Isaiah looked at Gramms, and she returned the same gaze back. He shook his head and walked away.

"You have to listen to your gut. You are the only one who can make this decision. This family bloodline has lasted as long as it can against the angels. They're getting craftier; they may show a general love interest in you, but I assure you, it is not." Gramms faded away.

Everything was left up to me. *How was I to decide which side deserved the Garden of Eden?* Sure, Gramms taught me the different creation stories than what the church does, but that doesn't mean it's true. It doesn't mean any of this is true. For all I know, there is no such thing as God, no such thing as angels or demons, well, Wanderers. I grew up listening to those stories and didn't want to believe in either side. Apparently, I was an ancient hag that held the key to the Garden, the key to the summit, and to guard both against the angels, which I have no clue why that would be important.

As I walked to my car, the skies began to darken, and I could have sworn I heard laughter in the wind. I reached for my car door handle, and my hand was grabbed. I looked up to see Dean holding my hand, preventing me from getting into the car.

"Well, I see the hag, and that annoying demon found a way to fill you in on everything. So, tell me, Guardian, where is the garden hidden?"

He wasn't smiling but rather sneering at me.

"You all are insane! There is no Garden of Eden, and it's not like I'm hiding it in my backyard!"

He glared at me and pulled me away from the car with strength I had never felt before. I stumbled to the ground and receded back on my elbows away from his face, with him still holding onto my arm.

"You will tell me where it is. I nearly had you pouring your guts out into my lap last time, and this time will be no different. Incaendiel may think he has the upper hand by growing up close to you and getting to know you, but he will not win! You may have been his zygote when he was in the summit, but he left you! He left you for darkness! I can give you light!"

I didn't know what to think. *He left me once before?*

"Oh, I can see those wheels turning. He has left you more than once, more than twice. There are millenniums of the same actions. His Dark Mother will not allow you two to be together. You will never be his!"

He still hadn't let go of my arm and was dragging me away from the car. My heart was thundering with fear. *Where was he going to take me? Was he going to torture the information out of me?*

"Let me go, or Isaiah will-"

"He'll what? Look around. He isn't here. He left you alone in the cemetery just as he did four years ago when they buried the old hag. You're coming with me!"

He was dragging me further to the center of the cemetery. *Was there a portal there or something? Oh God! I was sliding into their delusions now.*

"Let me go!" I screamed without realizing the power it packed.

He temporarily lost his grip, and I snatched my arm from his hand. I bolted for my car, and just as I took the handle, he hoisted me up at the waist. He continued to haul me, kicking and flailing back to the center of the cemetery.

"Isaiah, help me!" I screamed and kicked.

Dean laughed at my efforts and at my plea. We were nearly to the center of the graveyard, and there was no way I could escape his grasp.

"Incaendiel, save me!"

It was meant to be a silent plea, but I realized it was aloud. There was a crackle of lightning and thunder. In front of Dean, Isaiah stood with Sam,

Azazel, and Rafe.

"Drop her while you have a chance, Dean." Isaiah stood there with his fists clenched, ready to lunge.

"Four against one isn't much of a fair fight." Dean toyed with them.

"Oh, I can take you by myself," Isaiah spat at him. "Let her go!"

"You can try like you did last time."

Dean grinned at him. Something along the lines of a growl escaped Isaiah's throat.

"It seems Mama's Boy isn't going to let me grab and go this time," Dean said as he sat me down.

Within a split second, Sam was beside me, dragging me away from Dean. Isaiah stood there, staring down his target.

"You want to throw the first punch, or did Mother teach you to fight at all?" Dean smirked and looked at the three standing there. "We win this year, demons!"

With a blink of an eye, he was gone. There's no way someone can just disappear before your eyes. *I was going crazy! They were dragging me into their crazy delusions.*

I started to get dizzy and lightheaded. Everything was crashing down on me, and I had no clue what to believe. I slipped through Sam's fingers and hit the ground. I couldn't breathe, and the ground was spinning. *Was this a panic attack?* I had only heard them described to me. I had never experienced one before. I began choking back the bile rising in the back of my throat in between gasps of air. *It was all true. I can't believe it; it was all true. I was just getting ready to turn eighteen. I can't make a decision like this. This is not a decision for a human to make, let alone one that has barely made it into adulthood. This was the deciding factor of the war between the angels. What if I made the wrong decision?* I vomited and heaved up everything that was in my stomach, which was nothing but stomach acid. I blacked out. I heard murmuring in between the light and dark moments of my lucidity.

"I can't believe you summoned the old woman! What were you thinking!?" I knew it was Sam yelling. "When this mission is done this time, you will not be returning to help. I will make sure of that!"

No, no, you can't take my Isaiah from me. You can't take my Incaendiel.

CHAPTER 3

THE ANGELS GATHERED AROUND, waiting to see what news was being brought to them. Alpha appeared before them, looking at each and every one of them in the eye.

"Our universe is in trouble, children. By creating each of you, I have thrown the natural balance and order of the cosmos out of place. I never imagined my power would be so great to do this. I existed in the dark and brought about too much light. Now, I come before you to ask of you a simple request. Only the strongest and most powerful of you are up for the challenge." He glanced around at all his trophies of power. "Which one of you would wish to oppose me?"

The court remained quiet; not a single angel dared to oppose their master, whom they loved with their whole heart. "I need one of you to love me so much more than the others that you would give up your place here in the summit and become my Adversary. This does not mean you hate me; it just means we oppose one another with Light and Darkness to balance harmony." Still, not a single angel spoke up to take the test. Alpha became angry and impatient from the silence. "If one of you does not choose to do this yourself, I will command one of you to! I can call forth those of you I created with powers none other have!" The angels glanced nervously at one another. They did not want to give up their place in the summit nor become the Adversary of their father.

A melodic voice rang out through the court; it was a voice with such power that it brought tears to the eyes of the angels just from its sound. "My love, do not frighten the children." They immediately all felt safer and out of danger from the threat Alpha had just made.

"None of them will accept my request. What am I to do?" Alpha was perplexed and sat down on his throne. Omega sauntered up to him and touched his face.

She peered deep into his eyes, "You know I love you more than any of our children love you, right?"

"Of course, I know you do," he smiled back at her and touched her face back. A tear slid down her face, and it took him a moment to realize why..."No! I will not allow it!"

"I am the only one who loves you more than any other present in the court, which was your request. I will never hate you was another of the agreement. Why not me? Yin and Yang energies should be the Light and Dark of the Universe."

Alpha thought back to Tiamat and her words to him. She had sealed Omega's fate before him, and he had not even acknowledged it. Of course, the only power that would equal his would be his bride. He sighed heavily, but he knew this sacrifice was needed if he wanted to keep his authority and power over the universe. Without it, he would not rise to power like the others. "You are to take a few angels with you for protection."

"I cannot take our children from their home. They must choose on their own to leave the light and fall into darkness," she said as she walked to the Gate of the Summit. "Who shall go with me?" she asked, looking at all their faces. She could understand the torn look they had. None of them wanted to go and didn't want her to go either. It was heartbreaking for her. These were her lovely children, and she wished they would all go with her. "Do not feel guilty if none of you wish to go with me. I understand."

She turned to walk away when one of the angels burst forth in front of them. "I will go with you, my Omega, my mother. Father may have been the beginning, but you will be the end." She didn't even have to turn around to know whose voice it was. "Samael, my son, do any others follow you?" Samael turned and stared at his brothers and sisters. "Who shall follow?" Many stood still and glanced between themselves, and then another angel stepped forth. "I will join you, my brother." It was Azazel.

Once Azazel had stepped forth, it was easier and easier with the angels' choices until they were at half-and-half. "One thing you must realize, my children, is that this decision is permanent. You will be stripped of the light within your heart, the exceptional light that binds you to the summit. I will always love you all, but you may never return to your home again," Alpha said with a lump in his throat. "I hope your love for me never dies, and you never forget the real reason as to why you aren't here any longer. You all chose to leave. I did not make any of you do it. Therefore, you will be known as the Fallen Ones. You will keep your grace, but you will be forever changed."

Each of the angels that chose to fall nodded to their creator, their father, and they all jumped from the summit. They barreled straight toward the human world without lifting their wings once. The closer they came to Earth without opening their wings, the less light they held in their hearts. Their wings began to burn and blacken as they fell and sped toward Earth. They watched as their lustrous skin began to lose its sparkle. The Technicolor reality they were accustomed to began to erode from their sight. They looked no different from those of the human world, with their luminescent skin gone. The wonderful, silvery, blue eyes they had begun to blacken over to look like the sea during a storm. Their blonde hair turned to a dirty brown like a chestnut stallion. They were no longer the beautiful, graceful creatures they had once been, but they were still beautiful, nonetheless.

Omega was the last to take the plunge. She looked at her co-creator and smiled, "Let us hope it is not you who forgets to love us." She turned away from him, opened her arms, and free-fell through the blackness. Being a goddess and not one of the celestial creations, she did not lose her grace nor her light. She did, however, bury the light deep within herself. Since they were no longer the Alpha and Omega, no longer arm in arm with each other, she decided to take a different name that better suited her new self. Just as her fallen children looked, she too experienced a change of features except her hair turned a shade so black, it put the darkness of night to shame. Her eyes looked like the night sky, and her skin was the creamiest shade of white. She decided her name would be Lilith, the Dark Mother. When she landed amid the scattered fallen ones, they all gathered around her.

"My children, you will never be forgotten nor unloved, but you will never be the same again. It saddens me to see you in the shape that you are, and now, I wish I had not asked any of you to come with me. You will never be as you once were, full of light and iridescent beauty. As your creator, I am ashamed to see that I have caused this irreversible change to you. As your mother, I am heartbroken that I could ask such a thing of you to come with me, even if you fell by choice. Make yourself available to the humans as though you were still in the summit. For the time being, I will be alone."

She turned and made her way towards the Garden

of Eden while all her children stood with tears in their eyes. It seemed as if no one was happy over the plunge. They all separated and went to their normal human assignments to watch over them. The mother stayed in the Garden of Eden, the closest thing she had to her celestial home. She spent a lot of time with Adam. He reminded her of the happier times she had when she was in the summit with her Alpha. Adam saw how sad she had become, and it broke his own heart. He began to pay closer attention to her to cheer her up, ignoring his other creator. This made Alpha bitter and jealous. How could she steal what he helped create as well? It enraged him. So, when night fell, he slipped down to the Garden of Eden, removed Adam's memory of the mother, and placed it within the Tree of Knowledge.

Adam awoke to Alpha, giving him a new rule to live by.

"My dearest son, I have watched you sleep and have grown fond of your presence among my favored animals. I have created for you whatever your heart desires to eat and drink. However, the tree that grows beside the Tree of Life is forbidden to touch." Adam looked to the tree Alpha referenced. "This is the Tree of Knowledge," Alpha told him. "Fear nothing in this Garden, but I do bid you a plea. Whoever enters this Garden, if they do not shine like your guardians, do not speak to them. They will deceive you in any way they can think of. They may come in the form of your guardians, or they may come in the form of a beautiful woman, but they bear false love for you. Do you understand?" Adam nodded his head. "Good, now sleep, my son."

When Lilith entered the Garden the next morning, Adam was scared of her. "Why do you shy away from me, my son?" Lilith asked.

"I have but one creator, and you are not him. Who are you?" he asked, stepping away timidly.

"I have only been gone one night, and you do not remember who your mother is?" Lilith asked, pained.

"As I said before, I have no mother, only my father, Alpha," replied Adam. "He said someone might come and stake a claim as one of my guardians."

Lilith's eyes clouded over, and she glared at Adam. "You do not remember me at all!" she hissed.

"I would never forget such a beautiful face, even if you are evil," Adam said, stepping back with a fearful tremble. "Please, leave me be."

Lilith balled her fists and screamed, "ALPHA!" Adam retreated and ran to safety. The Fallen Ones gathered on the outside of the Garden where they could see and hear everything. Alpha descended in a white, luminescent light with his warrior angels at his flank.

"My love, Omega, how are you, my dear?" he asked snidely.

"Why does our creation remember me naught!? What have you done!?" she hissed so loud the earth shook.

"I removed his memories of you. You spent so much time with him in the Garden; he was beginning to love you more than me," he replied.

"You jealous, Cretan!" she screamed. "This was all your idea! You decided to create an adversary, and the only one able to do it was your wife. This was your fault! If you had visited your creations instead of hiding behind your guarded gates, they might have loved you as an equal, but it takes more than just creation to show love!" Lilith paced back and forth in anger. She glared at her lover, her forlorn husband. "You wanted an adversary? Well, now, my Love, you have one! The Earth is MY domain. You can fill it with as many human souls as you wish, but they must be born and not made. It takes both of us to create a human from nothing, and I refuse to help you. This planet will be under my rule. If you try to invade my domain, there will be a war that I'm sure you do not want your children involved in."

"They made their decision when they joined you, my dear!" Alpha shouted in retort.

"This is the only common ground we shall have to meet as it is the direct gateway to the summit. I have seen what the future holds for Adam. You removed me from his mind; therefore, he will become extremely unhappy and yearning for companionship. Since you do not contain the power we do together, you will have to create his mate, Eve, from his rib, sealing me in their offspring. Once they leave this precious Garden, it will be removed from its position and hidden." She scowled at him.

"That's not fair at all, my Love, for you to know its new location but not me," Alpha replied coldly.

"Neither of us will know the new location. I will choose a family lineage that will hold the secret of the Garden. They will keep the location secret to whatever extent they see fit. This family will be called Guardians. Every one thousand years, you may send an angel to search for the hidden location. To gain the knowledge from the family, your angel may take measures deemed fit. However, the slaying of the family is out of the question. Just to make sure no angel steps out of bounds on the journey their FATHER sends them on, I will send one of my Fallen Ones as well to oversee the family's safety." Lilith finished, staring at the Alpha.

"And if my angels are able to get it out of the human, what does that mean?" Alpha asked.

"The Garden becomes your Garden. We will no longer interfere with humanity and shall retreat into the dark as you wish. However, if the human tells my Fallen Ones first, then we will have limitless access to the summit, fallen or not."

"Deal! So, what is it that our creations do to anger

me that it would cause them to be banished from the Garden?" he chuckled.

"They eat from the Tree of Knowledge, where you have hidden my memory," she stated pragmatically.

He quit chuckling. "They will never remember they had a mother. I will always see to it that humanity forgets you and sweeps you under the Earth!" he sneered.

"We shall see, Alpha," she said, bowing and leaving the Garden. The light disappeared as well as Alpha and his warriors. The fallen angels gathered around their mother. She still had tears that dripped from her eyes. Everywhere a tear dropped, a weeping willow sprang from the ground. The tears rolled into a puddle, and the earth trembled as a trench formed. Her tears filled the trench, creating a lake.

"I thought he said he would always love us?" Samael stepped forth, asking. "Why did he stand there and mock our fall? It was he who asked us to join you, Mother. Did he ever love us to begin with? He never fought for any of us who stepped forth to stay! Was his love never there!? Or was it just you, Mother, loving us enough for both of you?" Samael slipped to his knees in despair and tears. The other fallen ones all took to their knees as well in tears. The blatant truth coursing through their veins; they would be Godless; they would be without a father that loved them; they would be bastards that he would make sure never saw the light again.

"My son, I shall never know if his love was ever sincere to any of you or even me," she said as one final tear slid from her eyes. This tear, however, did not grow a weeping willow in its spot. It grew a mountain. The mountain rose in leaps and bounds. At the base was a cave entrance, and she motioned all her children to follow her. The cave led to a stairway that descended into dank darkness. The further they walked, the darker it became. She stopped and snapped her fingers. A light arose in the darkness, and they found their own summit on Earth. They called it the Glade.

Unlike the hellfire and brimstone stories that had been told generation after generation, the Adversary did not live in what most people refer to as "Hell." Why would someone so loving want to live in darkness when it had already seized her heart? She succeeded in becoming the Adversary of Alpha through darkness, but darkness attained from his actions, not her actions. He caused her heart to seize up to prevent it from loving anything else ever again.

The Fallen Ones seemed to enjoy the Glade more than they had their home in the stars. Most of them had been archangels and a few sentinels from the other hierarchies, so they didn't get to stay in the summit. They had their daily assignments to attend, spending less and less time in the summit.

"My children, please gather around," she called out to all her followers. "There will be times when you feel yourself slip into darkness." She looked them all dead in their eyes. "This will not be your fault but mine alone. I asked you to fall, to lose your light, and I am the one to carry that burden. The one thing I ask of you is not to let this darkness consume you entirely. I may handle the darkness within my heart; however, you are not as strong as me. If you let it seep into your heart, you will not return from it so easily."

"We will never succumb to the envy and greed that our father has," Azazel stated as she lowered her head.

"That is good to hear, my dear, sweet Azazel, just heed my warning. Your father may have given you the titles of the Fallen Ones, but that is not what he intends to really call you. In my eyes, you are Wanderers, here to explore the darkness and to seek the light. In his eyes, you will become demons, vile creatures that he will convince humanity are against them and not out to help them. You will be viewed as wicked, dark, and evil because of your choice to follow orders. Through the years, you will learn and gain vast knowledge about the difference between the darkness and the light, and I hope they change your outlook on our situation. This is a blessing, not a curse."

"Are there any rules you are to lay down, Dark

Mother?" Samael asked, peering up to his sole ruler.

"Yes. You are to never harm a human. If word gets back to me that you have, I will strip you of your grace, and you will roam the earth as one. In the future, one of your brothers will be sent to walk the life of a mortal man. We are to help his cause, for he is deceiving the father and trying to bring the mother back into the light. Afterward, even though he will ascend and be punished, Lucifer will join our ranks."

A hushed murmur filled the ranks of the Wanderers. "Are you sure, mother? He is Second in Command of the Archangels. Why would he turn on Alpha?" Samael asks.

"For one, he is outraged over the situation; for two, Metatron would not accept the task. Your brothers and sisters have not forgotten you, and they are really angry with Alpha. They will do whatever it takes to save your grace and return your light." Lilith responds.

"Mother, how do you know this?" an angel asked, walking from the back to the front. Most of the angels had been silent throughout the whole speech, with the exception of Samael and Azazel, who were first and second in command.

"You already know the answer to that, Incaendiel, as you already know how the future looks with either the failure or success of your brother, Lucifer." She walked to Incaendiel and brushed her hand

I AWOKE with a pounding headache in total darkness. I figured I would be back home, and all this would have been one huge nightmare. That was not the case. I sat up and looked around, trying to focus in the dark to see where I was. I was still in the freaking graveyard.

"Those assholes left me here!" I was irate, scratch that, furious. I tried to stand but still felt dizzy, so I decided against it until the ground quit spinning. "I can't believe he left me again," I muttered.

"Who left you?" The voice in the dark scared the crap out of me.

I glanced around nervously, and my eyes adjusted to the figure that was sitting just a few feet away from me on a bench.

"I hope you didn't imply that I would just leave you in the middle of a graveyard passed out. That wouldn't be very chivalrous of me." He walked closer, but I already knew who the voice belonged to.

"So, what do I call you?" I asked groggily as I tried to stand again. I still wasn't able to stand up.

"Isaiah is fine," he said, reaching for my arm to help me stand.

"Well, you didn't come when I called for Isaiah. You only answered to Incaendiel." He flinched when I said that. *Good, he did have a heart.*

"What all did he tell you about yourself...about

me?" He was beating around the bush, and I knew exactly what he wanted to know.

"Well, let's see; apparently, we're angelic lovers, and you left me for our mother. Kind of incestuous if you ask me," I said, beginning to walk away when he pulled me back.

"I didn't leave you!" There was so much emotion behind the simple statement. "You told me to go! You told me that you saw us being together again one day!" He was furious.

He breathed in a deep breath with his eyes closed, and when he opened his eyes back up, his look softened towards me. His hand tentatively reached for my face. I could see he was fighting the urge to touch it, to stroke it.

"You have no idea how hard it was for me to leave you behind."

I hadn't realized that I was leaning in closer to his face, and my breathing had sped up along with my heart. I had never been drawn to anyone like this before. I don't even remember us having this connection when we were younger.

It was crazy to believe that in the brief period of time we had been talking again, that I could think I was in love with him. This was real life, not Hollywood. However, we had always had a connection. When I broke my arm in sixth grade, he was waiting on the porch when I got home from the hospital with flowers, candy, ice cream, and a sharpie. He said everyone in town knew about it. It hadn't dawned on me that my breaking an arm would not have made gossip of the little town of New Salem.

"We're breaking all the rules by bringing up our true selves. I better get you home." He grabbed my hand to tow me away, but the energy radiated through our hands and into my body.

I couldn't bear it any longer. I pulled him to me and threw myself into him. I kissed him lightly on the lips, touching his face, feeling the electricity prick me here and there. He wrapped his arms around me, inviting my kiss, pressing his lips back against mine, and then he pushed me away. I didn't know what came over me. I have never acted this way before with anyone.

"No, no, Sophie! We can't do this. It's breaking all the rules! Please, please don't make me really leave you behind this time. I can't walk away from you again."

The tears caught in my throat. I had never felt this drawn to him, and it was just getting stronger. I wanted him in my arms. I didn't want anyone else to be in them. I wanted to be his, and it felt like he wanted the same thing until he pushed me away. My heart crumbled. *Does he not want to be with me?* I felt the tension slice through the air when I thought it.

"Well, what do you want me to do? Do you want me to give Dean a chance?" He stiffened when I said his name. His fists were clenched. "I would rather just be with you...I don't want to go without you near me anymore. These last four years have been torture! I've had no one...do I?"

"Those are the rules. He has to be given a chance to sway you to his side." His words stung.

I didn't know what love was, but I was pretty sure those electrical sparks and fireworks meant I loved Isaiah.

"We will always have a deep bond. They hope they can break our bond, break you, and bring you to their side. I don't want them to, but it was part of the pact made, and we never break a covenant pact."

"Are you sure he won't try to drag me to wherever he was earlier?" I feared where I might've ended up if I hadn't called out for him.

"He has been reprimanded for his actions today. He's supposed to be a good little boy from now on."

My heart was aching for him. I knew deep down that Dean would never penetrate what we had together. Even if it was just a few moments of a spark, I felt like it was years of love.

As if he knew what I was thinking, "Last time, you knew who we were together and still almost chose him. Our bond gets stronger with every reincarnation but weaker after your eighteenth birthday."

"Why?" I didn't understand why it would get weaker. *Why then?*

He paused. "Eighteen marks the year I left you to fall." He disappeared.

I was left alone in the graveyard. We were only eighteen when he left. *Does that mean that we were all frozen at that age? Were they forever frozen as eighteen years old because they left their other half in the summit? What happens when I turn nineteen?* All these questions I needed answered, and I doubted that he would be the one to answer them.

I walked to my car and got in without any problems this time. I started the engine and pulled out of the cemetery. I hadn't even noticed that Gramms' Bible was tucked away into the passenger seat. I raced home and prayed mom wouldn't be awake waiting up for me. To my luck, she was soundly asleep in her room. I walked to my room and flicked my desk light on. The only answers I could get were bound in the book that lay on the desk. I opened the book and flipped through the pages to the spot where Gramms had left off.

CHAPTER 5

*T*he Fallen Shed Tears

"THE ANGELS GATHER ROUND, as their world decays. Watching and waiting for the end of night and the beginning of day. Bound by oath forgotten within days, left to walk the earth in pain. Twilight locked in eternal damnation, the darkness swallowing their salvation."

"HOW DO YOU KNOW ABOUT SOPHIE?" Incaendiel asked, walking closer to his Dark Mother. "How do you know what her visions saw but not Father?"

"Even though he created me, he put more power within me than he realized. He does not have the power to see into the minds of his angels. I was the one who breathed life into each of you, so I have a connection with you."

"Sophie said that we would be together again. The vision she shared is hazy in my head and becomes even hazier as the days between us grow. What did she mean?"

All the angels stared as he asked the Dark Mother the question. He had no rank to even speak with her. Why was he not put in his place?

"You two share a bond unlike anything I have seen before. Some of the others have a connection with their chosen ones, but not as strong as the two of you do. You two are what we call twin flames. I split your soul when I created you two. You two will be the key to us returning to the summit one day." Everyone in the room sucked in a breath of astonishment.

"How will we be the key? I do not understand." Incaendiel sat beside the Dark Mother. He missed Sophie terribly. All the fallen ones began to weep as his pain radiated and coursed through their hearts. He looked up to the weeping faces. "How do they feel what I feel?"

"You are more powerful than what you believe. You must believe in yourself, my son. You have the power to project as well as take. Go ahead, try to take the pain you inflicted amongst your brothers and sisters." Lilith smiled and looked out to those weeping in sorrow. Incaendiel closed his eyes and breathed in deeply, breathing back the emotion he had welled up. The tears immediately stopped, and all the Wanderers stared at him. No one here, including Samael or Azazel, had this gift or effect on everyone.

"Sophie will be the key to the summit. She holds the power to return us all. That is why when I proposed there be a guardian, your father hid her and will be sending her as the guardian every one thousand years. Each incarnation, he will get closer and closer to receiving the knowledge of where the Garden is. However, each time, you will get closer to getting your twin flame back and us returning to the summit where we rightfully belong. I should have never agreed to the adversary role. I had no idea his intentions were like this." She bowed her head in defeat.

"I know what the human world will think of me, but that is why I slipped back into the Garden as a snake and told Eve to eat the fruit. He cannot hide the truth about me if it is buried within their mind and etched into their DNA. He was foolish to make that tree instead of doing away with the memory of me completely."

"How many incarnations will she endure before we can be together? When will we know that it's the final incarnation?" Incaendiel was full of questions.

"How old are you, my son?" He had thought they were all created at once because they all looked the same age.

"It has been eighteen years since my creation."

"Each incarnation, your bond will grow strong in the beginning, but once she hits her eighteenth birthday, that bond will decrease, making her more susceptible to the angels that pursue her. When she reaches her eighteenth birthday, and that bond doesn't decrease in the slightest, that is the year that we will triumph and return to the summit. She is literally the key to the Gate." All the Wanderers cheered when they heard this bit of information.

"What happens when she turns nineteen, and the other angels haven't been able to squeeze the location of the Garden from her?" Lilith remained silent for a few moments.

"Do you really want to know what will happen to her?" she asked, staring him deeply in the eyes. He nodded. "On her nineteenth birthday, something tragic will transpire to separate the two of you once again. Her soul will return to the summit, where your father will keep it locked up, safe and sound.

You will remain another one thousand years without her by your side." Her eyes were dark and gloomy.

"That's not fair! Why doesn't she get a chance at a normal life?" Incaendiel was enraged. Random fires began to surface and cast their hazy heat in all directions. Lilith placed her hand on his shoulder, and the flames receded.

"She is not a human soul. She has but one purpose, and Alpha sees to that."

"That is still dark on his part. She's not just a toy or a tool in a plot." The anger and pity coursed through his body. Most of the Wanderers had trickled out after the fire nearly set everyone on fire.

"My son, this was her proposal and idea to your father."

CHAPTER 6

Why don't you Stay?

"STAY with me through the night, as my eyes slip into slumber. Stay with me through the day as my mind begins to falter. My heart and mind are not one and only deceive each other. For my heart knows what is what, as my mind begins to saunter."

MY HANDS TREMBLED as I marked the spot I was at and closed the book. I knew the notion of my death had crossed my mind when I thought of what might happen when I turned nineteen. I just didn't think that would be the answer. Of course, deep down, I knew I was the one who had made a deal with God, Alpha, whatever you want to call him. The sun was beginning to peek above the horizon. I hadn't realized I had spent the entire night reading the bible.

I rubbed my eyes and went downstairs to make some coffee. I had to start my job today, and with everything weighing on my mind, I honestly didn't feel like working there anymore. *Why bother?* In a year, I would die. There's no need to save for college any longer. My fate was sealed. I wish Gramms had told me this little tidbit of information. She must have known I would find out eventually.

As I walked into the kitchen, I noticed that coffee had already been made, and a steaming cup of coffee sat on the table. I double-checked Mom's room and found that she was still sound asleep. My nerves knotted up, and I walked back into the kitchen. There was no note by the coffee. I didn't know if Isaiah had made it or if it was a notion Dean had in his mind to do for me. More than likely, the latter since Isaiah said he would be distancing himself from me.

Just the thought of him staying away more sent a

pain through my heart. It was like someone had their hand on my heart and would squeeze it every time I thought of his love. *See, there it goes again.* It felt like I had loved him for years. I was afraid of this feeling. I knew what happened to girls when they fell too fast and too hard; they would end up hurt eventually.

I picked up the cup of coffee and walked outside. It had been a while since I had sat on the front porch and drank a cup of coffee while watching the sunrise. My mom let me do it right after Gramms died. Of course, it started off as hot chocolate, then tea, and then finally coffee. I was distraught when she died. The wound was barely scabbed over because if I picked at it, it still bled. So, I changed my train of thought to something else. To my dismay, nothing else would come to mind aside from Isaiah. Tomorrow was my eighteenth birthday, and then, apparently, I would begin to forget Isaiah's love as soon as I remembered it.

"It sucks. I know." His voice didn't startle me nearly as bad as I thought it would. I was getting used to them just popping up out of nowhere.

"What if this time...I don't? What if I hold onto us?" He walked over and sat down beside me.

"I doubt it's this time. Every time you have gotten weaker and weaker after your birthday. It's like your soul is giving up on us being together."

He leaned forward and clasped his hands together, looking down at the porch. It must have been torture for him when he quit talking to me four years ago.

"Maybe this time is different?" I reached over to touch his hands, and he pulled them from me.

"Please, don't get my hopes up. Not again." My heart yearned to touch him. I could feel the intense pull to just reach out and touch his face.

"I want to see what we used to be like. Before the fall..." I knew he could let me see it.

"I'm forbidden to show you. It's against the rules."

He sat back in his chair. His leg was shaking like a nervous twitch. I could see that he fought with every ounce of himself to not touch me, to not make that connection. I ignored the rules, besides, they weren't my rules. I had free will; everyone knew humans had free will. I sat my coffee down and planted myself in his lap.

"Please, Sophie." I ignored his plea and leaned in for a kiss.

Our lips touched, and the same magnetism I felt yesterday radiated through my body. I could feel it vibrating through me. His hands couldn't resist me in his lap. They went to my back, pulling me in deeper into him. I could smell his true self. I smelled lavender, sage, and every sweet note mixed in it. He smelled so different than Dean did when he rolled the window down. He smelled exactly like I wanted.

His hands traced my back, and I dizzied under his

touch. I wanted so much more. He must've felt this urgency. He pulled me away.

"You're getting me in trouble. Trust me, I don't mind the trouble, but there are rules I have to follow." He pushed a strand of hair from my face.

I love you, Isaiah. I didn't want to say it out loud. I couldn't say it out loud. If I did, my heart knew that would be the day he did leave. I didn't want to tell him, afraid he would leave me.

"Wait to tell me that after tomorrow," he said, picking me up and setting me down in my chair.

Just as fast as he was there, he was gone. *How did he know what I was thinking?*

The rest of the day seemed to fly by. I called the bookstore where I had been hired and told them unfortunately, I won't be able to work this year. I just wasn't ready. They completely understood and said no worries. The job would be there all year if I changed my mind. Mom took me shopping, exclaiming how proud she was her baby was finally turning eighteen. I wanted to ask her so badly about what was happening, but I didn't know how she would react. Instead, I trudged along behind her from store-to-store shopping for my party tomorrow. She bought me new clothes for school, a new cell phone and an iPod for my birthday, and then we went out to eat. While we were eating, I hadn't even noticed Dean walk up to the table until I heard my mother acknowledge him.

"Hello, Dean. How are you adjusting to the move?" I didn't even move my eyes from my meal.

"It's going. Sophie showed me around yesterday, and I was acquainted with everyone." I lifted my eyes in anger at him. *Idiot!*

"Sophie hadn't even mentioned to me that you two got to know each other yesterday." My mother smiled at me with a smile that said, *once he leaves, you're spilling the beans.*

"I was actually coming over to ask Sophie if it would be okay for me to come to the party tomorrow." He smiled, looking at my mother, working his magic on her.

"The more, the merrier, sweetie. What do you say, Sophie?" She nudged me under the table, and I lifted my eyes to Dean.

His eyes twinkled today and looked different than yesterday. It was as if he genuinely wished to participate.

"Sounds good. Can't wait to see you there." I tried to sound as convincing as possible.

It worked for my mother, not sure if it worked for Dean.

"I'll be there." He smiled and walked away. *Was Isaiah, right? Would he really win my heart over the love I felt right now?*

"He's cuuute!" She smiled at me, hoping I would take the bait of conversation.

"I just don't know if he's my type. He's more of a bad boy type."

I looked off after him as he made his way out the door. He turned and winked at me. I wanted to scowl at him, but I knew my mother was watching.

"Bad boy? He seems like an angel to me." *If she only knew...*

The rest of the day was over before I could blink, and I found myself lying in my bed, unable to fall asleep. I climbed out of my bed and made my way to the window. My room was on the second floor, and occasionally, I liked to sit out on the roof and enjoy the night air. I shifted the window open and climbed out. I sat down and gazed up at the stars.

"Planning to leave me sooner than predicted?" Isaiah was at my side, sitting down with me. I nudged him with my arm. "I didn't take you for a jumper," he chuckled.

"In exactly five minutes, it will be my eighteenth birthday." We were both silent for a few seconds. "I'm glad you showed up. I wanted to spend the last few minutes I had feeling the way I do about you with you." I leaned my head against his shoulder, and he wrapped his arm around me, inviting me to his chest.

"I'm never too far from you. I'm always here watching you sleep, watching over you in general." We fell silent.

"It was you that carried me from Gramms' grave

home, wasn't it?" A look of guilt spread across his face as if he weren't supposed to have done it.

"I couldn't leave you there by yourself. It wasn't safe, not so close to the portal they have to the summit." I nodded my head. He has always been my silent guardian angel. He snickered.

"You can read my mind, can't you?" He didn't have to answer from his chuckle. "I knew it. You're the only one, right?" He nodded. "This explains a lot." It was nearly my birthday like 30 seconds left.

"You were the one who took my pain the night of Gramms' funeral, weren't you?" He didn't respond this time, not immediately.

"I gave it back to you little by little until you could handle it." It made sense. It's why I broke down at the grave. The seconds had ticked down to 10.

"Can I have one more kiss?" My eyes pleaded with his.

He was the one who leaned in this time and kissed me softly on the lips. It felt like we lingered there for an eternity. I dizzied under the feel of his lips. He pulled back just as the clock struck 12 a.m.

"Happy birthday, Sophie."

Just like normal, as fast as he appeared, he was gone. What I didn't expect was the pain I felt whenever he left to still be there. I climbed back in my window and lay down to go to sleep. I knew it had to be a fitful sleep because when I awoke, the bedsheets were torn off, and the blanket was thrown in the flow. I never remembered my dreams. It must be some sort of precaution, so I didn't give away any information. I didn't know.

I jumped in the shower and dressed in the new clothes mom had bought me for my birthday. The party wasn't until the afternoon, so I thought it would be a quiet morning with Mom, that is, until I heard two voices coming from the kitchen, along with laughter. I walked downstairs to the kitchen. I could smell the coffee Mom would have ready for me when she beat me to making it.

My blood ran cold when I saw Dean sitting at the table with Mom. There was a personal birthday cake with a single candle on the top of it to the left of him. It was obvious he was the one who brought it. I closed my eyes and sucked in a breath. This was something I had to do.

Mom looked up at me and smiled, "Well, there she is. Dean thought he would stop by before the party and take you to get some breakfast as a present." The look on her face said, *you better accept the offer, or you're grounded.* I groaned on the inside.

"Sounds like fun!" I tried to sound as chipper as I could.

"Just remember the party is at 2. Don't be late. You know it's rude." The warning on her face for being late was more severe than turning down the breakfast.

"Don't worry. I will have her back in time, I promise." He stood from the table with the cake in his hands and lit the candle. "Want to make a wish?"

The one wish that I wanted to wish I knew wouldn't happen because he wasn't a living person. I grinned at the idea of Dean dropping dead. Since I knew it wouldn't come true, I made the next best one. I wished for Isaiah.

We took my car since he didn't have one, obviously. Small talk didn't seem to be his forte, so I started the conversation. "So, how does this work? Do we date until I fall in love with you, forget my love for Isaiah, and then you gain the Garden? Or would I hold out and rather die? Or I hang onto the love for Isaiah, and you lose?" He scowled at me.

"I preferred the other you. Knights in shining armor were your flaw. I have no clue how to woo you now." So, he had been planning on trying to sweep me off my feet the way he had last time.

"You could try to be yourself, for one." I looked over and saw a glint flash through his eyes.

"I don't think you're into the bad boy thing." He wasn't lying there. I have never been drawn to the bad boy pretense, but there was a slight tug when I saw him and Isaiah show down as they did at the ball field yesterday.

"I would rather you be yourself than someone you're not. That's more of a turn-off than you being a bad boy." *Why was I giving him tips? Was this one of his powers? Manipulation?*

"Ah, so you still like being the damsel in distress but under the strong arm of a man?" *How did he know that!? Uh-oh.* I shouldn't have said anything to begin with. I eased the car into park at the diner in town and turned the ignition off.

We walked in and sat down to be waited on. He was actually nice looking. The eyes of the girls I went to school with pierced through me. Jealousy over me was a new thing. We placed our order and sat in awkward silence.

"This would be easier if you acted like you were at least interested in me." I looked over at him. My eyes found his, and an odd sensation tugged at my mind. I did sort of feel a little comfortable around him.

"This is just a lot to swallow in a couple of days. I went from having no attention from guys to being fought over."

I blushed from blurting it out to him. He leaned over the table and placed his lips against mine. I felt an intense feeling rush through my body. It was a simple kiss, but it felt familiar to me.

"If it weren't for this being a mission, I wouldn't use the tactics I have used before. I really am attracted to you, both the real you and the angel you." His thumb brushed the top of my hand. "I have to follow orders. I have to hate my fallen brothers. If it weren't for the decree, I would be doing anything I could to help them get back as well."

He switched seats and sat beside me. He looped his arm around my waist, and my heart sped up. I didn't know which part of me was having this response, the human me or the angel me. He leaned over and kissed my cheek. "You may not remember, but we did have something special once before." He whispered it so softly in my ear. He sent goosebumps up and down my arms.

I felt like I was lost in the moment. I never knew that this would feel so releasing. My studies had always been my priorities, so I didn't swoon over hot guys at school. Our food came, and we ate in silence, but the silence spoke in volumes. I felt a bit lightheaded around him. I guess this was the feeling most girls felt when they were on a date.

We finished our food and walked to my car. He wanted to take me to a scenic lookout. I turned here and turned there, and we stopped at a lookout point off the highway. I put the car in park and immediately felt his arms around my waist, pulling me into him. His mouth found mine, and I invited his kiss in. He moved his mouth to my neck, and I closed my eyes. My body was responding in ways I had never explored before.

His hand snaked its way up to my face and pulled me in for another kiss. I was enjoying the moment until Isaiah's face popped into my head. It was like everything came to a screeching halt. I couldn't do this anymore. Everything in me screamed no, but for some reason, I couldn't resist. *Was this him still?* His lips touched mine. It wasn't the same electric shock as Isaiah's kiss, but it still sent tingles and waves through my body. *So, is this what it's like to kiss another boy, or to kiss another angel?*

As much as I wanted to pull away, I couldn't. I felt guilty. I knew what I was doing to Isaiah, doing to the "us" that wanted to be together again. It was breaking me apart inside, but something still kept me from pulling away. He slipped his tongue into my mouth, which was a big no-no for me, and I still couldn't pull away. He had to be using mind manipulation. This is how he got to the me one thousand years ago. *Was I stronger than her? Could I hold out as long as she did?* I must be stronger because they would have known he had manipulated her.

His hand started to snake up my leg, and I still couldn't protest. *Oh, my God!* He's going to fondle me, and I couldn't even build up the strength to push him off of me. This was not what Incaendiel discussed with me before. This isn't free will. This was against my will. I began to push with my mind for him to stop. I was yelling and pleading for him to stop. I could sense he heard my pleas, but he pressed forward.

His hand slipped from my thigh and moved up

under my skirt. His other hand started groping my chest. I couldn't believe it. I was going to be molested by a freaking angel. *What kind of God presides over him?!* He would sacrifice the virtue of an eighteen-year-old to get information for a freaking Garden! A tear slowly rolled down my face as his hand went further, but slowly up my skirt, as if he enjoyed me squirming under his hand. The bad boy thing was a definite no that I should've kept my mouth closed about.

I couldn't take it anymore. I called out with my mind. *Please, Incaendiel!* No sooner had my mind flashed the name that there were tons of people standing around my car. When I looked up, though, we weren't at the lookout any longer. Somehow, he had made me think we were. We were really at the cemetery. The passenger door flew open, and Dean was yanked off me. My door flew open to hands, grabbing me and pulling me free from the trap I had been in.

"Dean, you're honestly using powers against her! Mind manipulation!? Is that what you did last time as well!?" It wasn't Isaiah or Sam yelling at Dean. It was another young man.

"Michael, I'm sorry. I had no idea I was doing it." His eyes bore fear within them.

"I call bull! Father wants to see you as soon as possible. Your trip is over this time!" The one called

Michael was furious. He snapped his fingers, and Dean disappeared. I buried my face into the chest of the person who pulled me from the car. I was so lost in the fear I had no idea who it was, but whoever it was, I was silently thanking them for ripping me out of the car at that exact moment.

"Sophie, I am truly sorry for the way he treated you. Do not be mistaken that this was in any way approved in the eyes of our father. Dean will be reprimanded to the highest measure." Michael was sincere in his words.

"It shouldn't have gotten this far, Michael. What if he had gone farther before she called out?! Lord knows what he would have done-" the voice stopped short. Anger tainted each syllable spoken. The voice I knew so well. The voice that sent ripples through every tendon and muscle of my body. My face flushed as I thought of him.

"We honestly had no idea this is what would have happened. Please forgive me, Brother, and forgive those who were a part of the idea, if any exist." Michael didn't act like all the other angels did. He wasn't rude or snide with them. Then it dawned on me.

"Michael...as in Archangel Michael, the angel of strength and courage?" His eyes widened a bit in surprise. "No, it's not a memory. My mother took me to church for a while, and you are in the Bible." His eyes seemed to relax.

"Yes, I am that angel." He smiled at me, and I could feel that he really meant his gesture. Another angel appeared to the side of Michael and whispered into his ear. "Father requests my presence. Zadkiel, will you see to it that no other tries what has transpired today in my absence." Zadkiel nodded while he stared at me. I didn't feel comfortable under his gaze. Michael broke the air, "Until next time." He bowed his head and was gone. Zadkiel had a look plastered on his face that I couldn't shake. His face seemed so familiar, but I couldn't place it.

"I beg your forgiveness for what my ignorant brother has done to you and for the quick departure of our second in command. What is a suitable gesture for this kind of action? Dinner, maybe?" I was about to answer when I felt Isaiah stiffen.

"Are you sure this wasn't planned so you could be the big hero in her damsel in distress situation?" It clicked with me there. The exact words that Dean had said to me.

"I assure you, Brother, that is not-" I interrupted him before he could finish.

"Choose your words carefully." Zadkiel eyed me, and I could see the facade beginning to lighten.

"Tell me, Sophie, what did that kiss with Dean feel like? Did you want more of it?"

I blushed. He made me feel like a whore in front of everyone standing around. I looked from Sam's face to Azazel's face. I didn't want to answer.

"That's all the answer I needed." He smirked at me and turned to walk away.

"I felt guilty for kissing him." I blurted it out, but it stopped him dead in his tracks. He whipped around, walked up to me and was inches from my face.

"What did you say?" His words weren't as kind as before.

"I-I said I felt guilty for kissing him." All eyes were trained on me, a look of surprise crossing Sam and Azazel's face.

"And why did you feel guilty for kissing him? Because he was an angel? Because it was your first kiss in public? Why!?" he yelled. He terrified me.

I was finally able to choke back the fear and squeak a response. "Because it wasn't Isaiah I was kissing."

It was barely a whisper, but everyone heard it, and I felt Isaiah tense even more. His grip tightened around me. I didn't know why until the angel lunged at me.

"You will give us the Garden! You will tell us where it is!"

Sam and Azazel were holding him back; well, struggling to hold him back was more like it. Isaiah never let me go but flew off with me into the wind. I could hear Zadkiel screaming,

"There will be court pulled for this, Incaendiel!

Your days are marked!"

It felt as if we were in the air for only a few moments, but we ended up miles away at a lake. Isaiah loosened his grip on me and turned me to face him.

"Tell me you're not lying to deceive the other side. It's not wise to mess with Zadkiel. Tell me!"

He was furious, and I was still scared from everything that had transpired. My eyes dropped from his to the ground from terror. He softened his gaze at me and lifted my chin so our eyes would meet. The eyes that stared down at me were the eyes I loved to see. So dark, like the sea.

"Tell me!" he pleaded, and I could feel his entire body shaking.

Instead of telling him, I pulled him close to me and planted my kiss on his lips. Our lips lingered forever on one another. The magnetic pull and electrical spark that was always there were stronger. He pulled me in tighter and kissed me harder. My body was completely melted into his. His tongue slipped into my mouth, but it wasn't like before with Dean. I wanted it. I craved it. My body asked for more; it needed more. Just as fast and long as the kiss had started, it ended. He pulled away from me. My entire body buzzed, and I could see a faint glimmer of light from his body. His eyes looked at me in surprise. I couldn't understand what he was surprised about. He should've been able to sense my emotions.

"What? What is it?" I asked in confusion.

"You're shining!" His eyes were wide in disbelief.

"Is that normal?" I asked, looking down at my hands. "Maybe it's because you are, too." He looked down at the faint glow of his hands.

"No, this isn't normal. This has never happened before." I was stunned. I didn't know what it was supposed to mean either. "I'm going to take you home before you are late for your party."

"Will you stay?" He closed his eyes, meaning no. "It would mean a lot."

"I have questions that need to be answered. I'm sorry." He picked my hands up and kissed them.

"Where are you going?" I asked, kissing his hands back.

Just the touch of his hands to mine made me crave him more and more. I didn't understand what was happening. People just don't fall in love overnight. It doesn't happen that way, but there was no mistake in the growing euphoria I had whenever I was around him.

"I'm going to send Sam and Azazel to watch over you in case they try to kidnap you and make off to the portal with you."

He grabbed me by my waist, and it took the breath from me. My heart thumped in my chest, and when I looked around, the lake disappeared. We were immediately at my house on the front porch. I turned to face him. I wanted to kiss him again; I needed to kiss him again. Sam and Azazel appeared immediately by his side.

"Watch her. Keep Zadkiel from her. I will be back later." He started to walk away when Sam stopped him.

"Where are you going?" It was a simple question, but it took a few seconds for him to answer.

"I'm going to see Mother." And like that, he was gone.

The other two just looked at me. They didn't just look at me; they looked me up and down.

"What?" I asked, blushing.

"After the party, we all need to talk." Sam was as serious as I had ever seen.

"Will the humans see her glow?" Azazel asked.

"Not like we do. There will be a glow about her, but it will just be like a happy glow. It bringing attention will be a different story. She hasn't had this glow since Mariam died."

CHAPTER 7

Feel the Burn

*F*eel the Burn

"THE LIGHTS ARE SWIRLING as the heart beats fast. Visions of love from days long past. Hope is mounting as the fear dissipates. Longing for the old-time ways. Her hand in his, his lips to hers, eternity waited for this moment of burn."

"INCAENDIEL, why have you left your assignment and come back here? You know you're supposed to stay until her nineteenth birthday. She's not safe without you by her side." I had barely made it down the spiraling staircase when I heard her voice.

"It's urgent, Mother," I replied, reaching the last step.

"What is so urgent that you-" she stopped midsentence while gazing at me. "Your light! It's faint, but there. How did you return it?" She walked over to me, examining my faint glow.

"It's the year, Mother." She stared at me wide-eyed.

"Are you sure? We don't want to get our hopes up this time like we did last time." She was watching my face for a hint of a response before I made one.

"The angels are going against the rules. Dean used mind manipulation on her last time and tried this time. She called out to me before he could do it for more than a day. He tricked her mind into it last time. This time, she is stronger and didn't give in."

"What did he try?" She eyed me curiously.

I held back the rage that coursed through me, afraid I would ignite the Glade again like I did so many years before.

"He tried inappropriate things with her, and she called out to me. The other team of angels were in league with his doings and were going to play the damsel in distress card on her."

My fists were clenched tight. It angered me that Zadkiel had been behind the scheme as well. I knew he was a snake, but I never imagined such a high-ranking angel would stoop that low.

"What did Zadkiel do?" She must've read my body language. Hell, she could've read my mind.

"She wouldn't fall for the damsel in distress card, so he asked her if she felt anything while kissing Dean." I paused.

"What did she say?" Mother had grown curious.

"At first nothing, he took it as a sign that they were winning again, but then..." I stopped again. I still didn't want to believe the truth behind her words.

"But what?" She was urging me to keep telling her.

"She said she felt guilty because it wasn't me she was kissing."

Mother turned from me. I knew she was thinking everything over in her head.

"The words mean nothing, Incaendiel. She has to show you she still loves you." Her voice was solemn.

"I whisked her away from everyone and told her that. That's when she kissed me. The same kiss we share every time after her eighteenth birthday has begun, but it was more powerful than I have ever felt it." I waited for her to respond.

"Is that when you began to glow?" Her voice was still unsure of everything.

"Yes, but-"

"But what!" she interrupted once more, this time a little bit angry. She still wasn't happy with my report.

"She was glowing too." She whipped around and faced me.

"You are sure! She began to glow as well?! You must be sure!" She walked over to me, her eyes dancing over my face for truthfulness.

"Yes, I'm sure. Samael and Azazel can attest to it. She's still glowing." I could see her thinking inwardly to herself.

"Do the angels know she is glowing yet? Have they seen her glow?" She was pacing the floor.

"No, but it won't be long before they do. We're going to keep her under our watch until it's time, just in case they try to kidnap her and pry the information out of her."

"Has she remembered where the Garden is yet?" That's a question neither of us have bothered to find out.

"She hasn't told me if she has." She didn't reply to my answer. "Is that a good thing or a bad thing?"

90

"I don't know my son, but we need the location of the Garden before we can reach the summit. Even with your light restored to full power, the only gateway we can use to get to the summit is the Garden. You have watched her all these years. Has she ever given any indication of where it's located?"

"No. It's been a long time since she has remembered our love since this began. I'm sure even her soul cannot remember, or for that matter, she may have moved it a couple of times as well." Her eyes darkened.

"I hadn't even thought of that." She was thinking to herself again. "From now on, Samael is to report to me anything of importance, and you are to not leave her side. Ever. For any reason, do you understand?" She caught my eyes, and I immediately understood why. I nodded at her. "It's time for you to return. Have Samael keep me posted." I turned to walk away. "Incaendiel?" I stopped and looked back at her. "You know the stakes. You must not get hurt. In your human form, anything can kill you, even if you have your powers. They are to protect both Sophie and you at all costs. Without your union as one, we cannot return."

My blood ran cold. They had nearly killed me last time, and luckily, it was on my last day as a human. Right before I passed, I returned to my normal form.

"Don't try to save her this time. If she dies, she will reincarnate. If you die...you will not." I swallowed hard and nodded my head.

Mother knew I would do anything to keep my Sophie out of harm's way, but I knew this time it was important. I had to protect her at all costs, but if I endangered myself, it would all be for nothing in the end. I mounted the staircase and popped out at the cave entrance. I wasn't expecting anyone to be standing there, but sure enough, Michael and Zadkiel with a crew of angels stood before me.

"You know you are forbidden to come to the mountain!" My words filled the air with heat.

"We were just waiting for you, Brother. Come, we would like to have a word with you about your concubine if you don't mind." Zadkiel grinned at me. I scowled at him.

"Brother, why do you talk to him with such malice?" Michael shook his head at Zadkiel's actions. "Please, Incaendiel, we do need to speak with you about Sophie."

"I am not going anywhere with you. We can speak here freely of the issue."

I sent a mental alert to all my brothers and sisters below the mountain floor, and there was a tremendous rumble. Behind me stood an army of my allies.

"Now, is that any way to treat a guest." Zadkiel snickered, and his eyes flared at all of us.

"You are not welcome here, Brother of Light!"

Zadkiel scowled at me and raced forward. He grabbed me by the throat.

"Brother of Darkness, do you wish to test my strength?"

His hand gripped tighter, cutting my breath off. It was against the rules to harm one another while we were in human form, but not a word was said to make him stop. What he didn't know was that I retained my powers while in human form. I grabbed his arm, and my hand superheated. He yelled, dropping his grip on my throat. He threw a punch that caught me square in the jaw.

"Enough, you two!" Michael's voice echoed through the valley. I wiped the corner of my mouth, where it had started to bleed from the punch.

"Do you wish to bring war upon Earth? I see your army behind you, waiting for the word. Why don't you say it and get it over with?" Zadkiel was testing me.

"That is not my call. They do not stand here to protect me; they stand here to protect our mother, or has Father brainwashed her from your memory as well?" I knew my words would sting.

"She was the one who abandoned us!" He was furious.

"At Father's request. He should have chosen his words better than he did."

I glared at him and felt the heat radiating from my body. I was only in my human form, but my powers were still damaging. I was one of the few angels who kept my power while in human form.

Zadkiel was fuming now. "She left us!"

"You had the chance to follow! You were too worried about leaving the summit or losing your light that you didn't care for her any longer! It was your choice to stay! She loves us all and still does! That's what you don't understand. Father no longer cares about those who fell with her, but she still loves each and every one of you that remained behind!"

"If she still loved us, she would return!" Zadkiel stared me down.

"What do you think we're trying to do? She doesn't want to abandon those of us who were faithful to her and return without us." I wasn't sure if I should have blurted that out. Michael, however, did become more attentive to the conversation.

"How can you return after you fell? You have no light left." His eyes studied me, waiting for my answer.

"Maybe one day, when I know I can trust you, and it's not a ploy to get the Garden, I might tell

94

you. Right now, I have orders."

He stared at me for a few moments. I didn't know if it was the heat boiling beneath my skin or if he knew he and I would truly talk alone in the future, but he seemed to change in demeanor.

"It's time to return to the summit. Maybe we can catch this chat at a different time." Michael signaled for them to follow him as he swooped through the sky.

Zadkiel scowled at me and then disappeared behind the rest of them. I turned to the army that stood behind me. Their eyes watched me in awe. I knew what they were thinking. No one had ever stood up to Zadkiel or tested Michael like that aside from Samael or Azazel.

"Thank you for standing behind me." They disappeared below the mountain, and I knew it was time for me to return to Sophie.

The year ahead of us was going to be treacherous waters. We didn't know where we stood. Lucifer had yet to join our side of things. It had been two reincarnations already since he was forced upon the cross. I didn't know if he changed his mind about things or if he was just waiting for the right time to leave and join Mother. I knew she had been sullen for the last 2,000 years since he didn't immediately fall into rank on our side. Maybe Father knew of his plot to join our side, and he is imprisoned in the summit until he reforms.

Either way, the addition of his power to our mission was thwarted.

I arrived at Sophie's house just as the party began. Her mother let me in, and I walked the all too familiar halls of the house. We walked down to the basement where the party was at. Her mother pointed her out to me, and I nodded, smiling, giving my thanks. She looked so beautiful. Her human incarnation was the closest it had ever been to her angel form.

You have no idea how hard it was to refrain from talking to her for the four years I did. Her Gramms, Mariam, was already filled in with everything when we arrived as young children. All four of us stayed with her as her foster children so we could keep an eye on Sophie. Samael claimed we were getting too close to one another and breaking the rules. So, I told Mariam I couldn't be around whenever Sophie was around. She understood the importance and the rules surrounding the situation. She told me not to worry, though, that this was the year that changed everything. I guess she was right.

I made my way over to the present table. I contemplated putting my present there for her, but I didn't want her to be embarrassed in front of everyone after opening it. I would wait until we were alone, and then I would give it to her. I looked around the room at everyone who was there. I recognized everyone from school, which was a good thing. There weren't any party crashers here, so her party could ride along smoothly. I mingled with a few people, joking and listening to the gossip of the town. I still hadn't laid eyes on Samael or Azazel. They were supposed to have been watching her closely.

I slowly made my way over to her. I didn't know if her light would brighten and be noticeable when she saw me. My eyes were trained on her face. She was smiling and laughing, something I hadn't seen her do in a long time. It was like she was at peace on the inside. As if she felt my stare, she glanced up at me. Her eyes connected with mine, and I felt the intense pull to her I had always felt. She smiled sweetly at me and blushed slightly. I always loved seeing the rush of heat to her cheeks. In those few seconds, it felt like the world stood still between us. Nothing else in the world mattered to me except her eyes looking deeply into mine.

I kept my distance the entire time, making sure we didn't stir any rumors among the people at the party. The cake came; she blew out all the candles, and slices were passed around to everyone. I kept to myself most of the time. I didn't know if I would give anything away if I talked to anyone. Everyone was used to me being silent around them anyway.

The entire party she kept glancing over at me with her eyes. Her eyes were full of everything that I yearned for. I missed the passion we held together before the fall.

She opened her presents and thanked every person who brought her one. She seemed kind of glum that they ended. I knew she was hoping to get one from me. I smiled to myself. I just knew this was the year. It would be the final year of all this battling over her would to come to an end. Everyone began to slowly trickle away, going home. She expressed her thanks to everyone who had come to the party. Soon, it was just her and me left alone in the room. The music was still playing, and a slow song had begun to drift from the speakers. I slowly made my way over to her, and she followed suit, meeting me in the middle of the room. No words were spoken; they didn't need to be. I took her in my arms and began to sway with her to the music. She laid her head on my chest and breathed deeply. I knew she could smell my scent, the scent that was unique to every angel.

We held each other in the middle of the floor, her head on my chest, my chin nestled on her head. I had waited centuries for this moment. She moved her head back from my chest and looked up at me. I knew what she wanted. It was the same thing I wanted. I leaned in to kiss her when we were interrupted.

"So, this is the reason you didn't want to go out with Dean this morning. You should have told me, sweetie." Her mom stood there, smiling, watching the two of us. Sophie's face went completely red, and I had to stifle a laugh.

"Mom!" I could see from her tomato, red face that she was completely without words in front of her mom.

"You two should go catch a movie together." She winked at me, and I nodded my head back as a reply. I looked down at her face and murmured, "Sounds like a good idea."

"I'll clean up down here. You two go! Have a fun time!"

Her mother had always been a sweet person. It was such a shame that Sophie's father had treated her the way he had. I led her by the hand to the steps and up out of the basement.

"So, do you want to go watch a movie? Or do you want to go somewhere else?" She peeked her eyes up at me and cocked a sly grin.

"Anywhere?"

I sighed, smiled, and shook my head at myself. I opened the rabbit hole.

"Yes, anywhere."

She grinned ear to ear at me.

She wrapped her arms around my waist and whispered, "Take me to the lake." I smiled.

In a flash, we were there, still standing, holding each other. She moved her eyes to look up at me and smiled. Her light began to glow again. I couldn't resist the temptation this time and leaned down, planting my lips onto hers. No one else could smell her scent but me. I had asked for centuries, but everyone had always denied she had her angelic smell. The lavender crept into my nose, followed by a rosy, floral scent with warm vanilla hues. I shuddered; the smell and the ripples sent goosebumps over my body. My hands roamed every inch of her back and made their way to her face and hair. I slipped my tongue into her mouth and felt the heat of her skin beneath my hands. Her hands searched my back and sides with fierce strokes. I could feel how badly she wanted to go further than just kissing.

I pulled back from her and saw the burning in her eyes. They were smoky and tinged with fire. She was getting closer and closer to her angelic self.

"As much as I would love to ravage your body on this boulder, we have a few things we have to do before we can do that."

It took a few moments before her eyes went to their normal indigo color. I could feel the heat subside, and her cheeks went to a normal color. But what hit me in the stomach was the sad look she gained afterward.

"What's wrong? I didn't mean to sound so business-like if that's what it is." She shook her head, and I could see she was fighting back the tears. "Well, what is it then."

I lifted her chin to see her eyes. Her angelic powers were running rampant. Her eyes looked like an ocean's waves crashing on the beach.

"I was hoping that...well...never mind."

She bit her bottom lip. It dawned on me she had the same look at the party when she finished opening her gifts.

"You were hoping I had gotten you a gift, right?"

She squinted her eyes as if thinking, "How did he know that?" I chuckled and fished the gift from my pocket. I handed it to her, and she took it carefully. She had no idea what was inside the tiny little box. I could sense her heartbeat had hastened. She unwrapped the paper and stopped before she opened the box. I knew she was afraid of whatever would be inside the box. She opened the box and took in a slight breath. It was an ancient bracelet that I modified to look more modern. I had added angel charms to it, but I didn't destroy the originality of it. On top of the bracelet were symbols that only angels knew how to decipher. It was the language of the angels that historians call Enochian.

"I... I remember this bracelet." My heart nearly stopped.

"What?" I asked. It was impossible for her to remember the bracelet.

"I remember this bracelet," she restated what she had said more matter-of-factly.

"It's not possible." It came out in a whisper.

"I gave this bracelet to you." The world around me seemed to stop spinning. *How could she remember that?* After all the reincarnations and being locked up—only Alpha knows where—to not remember anything...how could she possibly remember that?

"Do you remember when you gave it to me?" I knew it was a long shot, but I had to know how far her memory had resurfaced.

"I gave it to you the day you fell." My entire body was enraptured in chills, and I nearly passed out.

"What do the symbols mean?" I asked, barely choking out the words.

"What symbols? It says, 'together forever.'" I jumped up, nearly toppling her over. "What? What's wrong?"

"It's impossible for you to be able to read that! That's the angelic language. Only we angels can read it!" I was pacing back and forth. I didn't know if this was a good or bad thing. "What else do you remember?"

"I remember being summoned forth in front of Alpha and asked to perform a task." Her eyes grew dark.

"What was your task?" I was in pieces waiting for her response.

"He told me to stay away from you. Your agenda was not a holy one...you were trying to steal the Garden of Eden from him." She stood to her feet and began to back away slowly.

"No, no, no. He implanted the evil behind it." I could see it in her eyes, though. She didn't believe in the good in me any longer. "Please, Sophie, I've waited centuries to give you that bracelet. Don't shut down on me, I beg you."

"Why should I listen to you?! Alpha knew how much it tore me when you left me to follow HER! You abandoned me for the dark! Alpha told me if I kept the Garden from you, I would stay in the light even when you would be swimming in the dark!"

"He lied to you, Sophie! God-damn! I shouldn't have given it to you. I knew he had something to do with messing with your memories. I didn't abandon you! You told me to go! This whole thing was your plan! It was your vision! He's turning it around on you. You have to believe me, Sophie."

Tears began to brim behind my eyes. My emotions began to surge through my powers.

Fires began popping up everywhere, along with rain tearing through the sky. The forest caught fire and began to slowly cease to exist. I ran my hands through my hair as the rain soaked me. I was defeated. This is why they were never worried about us getting the Garden. They had brainwashed her true self into thinking we were evil, that we were no longer one of them. *How could he do this?! How could he truly abandon his children over a stupid Garden?!*

I felt a hand on my shoulder. "My son, come out of this dark hole you have formed."

I looked up to see Mother standing there. Behind her stood Samael and Azazel, along with Sophie. She was soaked from head to toe from the rain, and her eyes were wide with fright. Samael and Azazel even kept their distance.

"We will never reach the light. Why struggle against the darkness?" My heart was ripping in two.

"What makes you think you will never reach the light, my son?" Mother sat down beside me at the edge of the lake.

"Father has made sure of it. All these centuries of trying to get her to remember my love, he was up there, brainwashing her into believing we were truly evil now. She doesn't remember the vision; all she remembers is what Alpha put in her mind."

104

I sniffed. The tears had already fallen, and just as Mother's tears, a weeping willow stood where each tear fell.

"What your father had not counted on was not her will, but your will. I don't know if you realize, my son, but you are much more powerful than any of your brothers or sisters. Your power mounts the longer you are with her. The two of you are the most powerful combination since your father and me. You must not lose the hope we have clung to for so long. Her true memories will surface in due time." She kissed my forehead and stood.

"I don't know how much longer I can fight the darkness. I don't know how much longer I can wish for the light without it within me. I'm not strong like you, Mother. The more I try to reach the light, the more I am enraptured by the dark. What would happen if I just finally accepted it?" I didn't even look her in the eyes when I asked the question, for I already knew the answer.

"We're so close to home, Incaendiel. Please, my son, keep your head above the putrid waters." She was gone.

No more questions and answers. I sat at the edge of the lake. I didn't move. I didn't want to move. It was hard enough just to fight the black cloud hovering over me. I couldn't look over my shoulder at the three of them standing there. I was ashamed of my actions and too grief-stricken.

"Are you going to take her home?" Samael asked, breaking into my darkness.

I swallowed the lump in my throat and fought the tears back from brimming over again. "Could...could you...I can't right now...I-" I felt a hand on my shoulder. It was Azazel.

"Don't worry, Brother. We will take her home and guard her until you return."

CHAPTER 8

All is Perceived in Darkness

"THE DARKNESS CONSUMES the soul unlit by heavens waking grace. An unlit soul is hard to save from the abyss of fiery rain. Accept the darkness in your heart or forever walk in between. Darkness is just the night of day the light is forever just a dream."

"IS IT TRUE?" Azazel asked as we both got ready for bed.

She was sleeping over with me tonight; Mom was thrilled. I never had friends over anymore. Azazel and I had been close when we were younger. When Isaiah stopped hanging out around me, we drifted apart. I wasn't sure why, but we did.

"Is what true?" Neither one of us had really spoken since the lake. I had never seen Isaiah so upset, so disturbed.

"That Alpha told you we were against those that remain in the summit."

I really didn't want to talk about it. "That's what I remember." I wasn't in a talkative mood and really didn't want to discuss what had caused Isaiah to flip out and nearly burn the planet down.

"Do you believe it?" *Did I believe it?* After hearing Isaiah talk to me and then seeing the Dark Mother appear, I didn't know what to believe.

"I don't know." We were both silent for a few moments. "What did Isaiah mean by not being able to fight the darkness any longer?" I heard her take in a deep breath and release.

"When we fell with Mother, we lost our light. Our light is what kept us pure, kept us from susceptibility to evil. The longer we're from our light, the weaker our fight against the dark is. We've lost many brothers and sisters to the struggle where the darkness won. They were cast out to walk through the world for all eternity, alone. Those of us who remain have fought long and hard against the temptation of the dark. None of us, however, have fought as hard as Incaendiel has against the darkness. It weighs heavier and heavier on him each time you are incarnated. I guess it was Alpha's plan to use you. Our only key into the summit is you, but it is through him as well. If we lose him, we lose all hope. Up until the last few days, the darkness was suffocating him." She stopped for a minute and then looked at me. "And then you came back into his life. I saw the light in his eyes, and then I saw the light radiating from his body. It was casting the darkness aside." She fell silent.

"What did you see today when you reached the lake?" I asked it without thinking.

She looked at me. "Even though he still has traces of his light, there is a dark cloud that has completely engulfed him. The only thing keeping the dark from completely taking over him is his hope and..." she paused.

"And what?" I asked.

"His love for you." I stared at her as she stared back at me. "We all felt his cry. He has always had that sway over us. Whatever emotion he feels that is immediate and unbearable to hold in, we all feel it. Mother felt it this time."

I was silent. I didn't know what to say. *Sorry?*

109

Sorry for telling him what my memories told me?

"We're so close to the light this time, Sophie. We just want to go home! It's a catch-22. The closer we get to the light, the closer he gets to the dark. Each incarnation of yours, I see it consuming him more and more." She paused as if she were going to say something.

"What?" I asked.

"It's nothing. Just a thought, or rather, fear." She shook her head and smiled.

"What?" I asked again.

She sucked in a breath, "I think at the last moment, when we have won and are returning to the summit full of light, he won't. I'm afraid, at the last moment, as the last person to climb the rainbow bridge, he will lose himself completely to the dark. It would be ironic, really, that the one person who could get everyone into the light would be the one that darkness consumes. I don't know. It's a fear I have voiced with Mother." She sat in the chair at my desk, fiddling with her hair.

"What did she reply?" My voice was barely a whisper. I could see her choke back the emotion.

She cleared her throat. "She said...she feared the same thing for him."

I bit my lip, fighting back the welling emotions behind those words.

"So... ahem," I cleared my throat, trying to fight

choking on the words. "So, he will make sure every one of you gets through before he lets the darkness subdue him?"

"I don't know. I don't know how any of this is supposed to work. I don't know if he has the actual power to call down the Rainbow Bridge or what. All I know is that it is up to you and him to save all of us Wanderers and to return our light."

"What happens to one of you if you die here on earth? Are you like me? Will you reincarnate?" Azazel wouldn't even look me in the eyes for an answer. "You die, don't you." It was barely a whisper.

"That's enough chit-chat. You need to get some sleep." She offered a smile, but I saw the sadness behind the smile.

I wished I hadn't said the things I had to Isaiah. I was propelling him further into darkness, which was not a good thing. My entire existence on the planet had caused him to slip further into the darkness, nearly surrendering himself to the cold of the dark. He was completely selfless, whether it be to keep me safe or for his brothers and sisters to cross the bridge.

This whole roller coaster of emotions had me spiraling out of control. One minute, I would hate him; the next, love him and then want to die. I wondered if it was my angelic soul colliding with my mortal body as it tried to surface. I slipped under the comfort of my comforter and drifted off to sleep. For the first time in eighteen years, it wasn't just a sound sleep. I began to dream.

I saw myself, but at the same time, it wasn't me. This girl was exceedingly more beautiful than I could have ever been. She stood with Isaiah, but she called him by his real name, his angelic name.

"Incaendiel, you must go with Mother or the others will be lost." She looked at Incaendiel as all the angels lined up to go with Mother.

"Why does it have to be me? Why does it have to be us?" Incaendiel didn't like the idea she had told him, well rather, the vision.

"We share the strongest bond than any other here." She looked deeply into his eyes. "I do not have your strength or your will. I will not be able to persevere as you would. You would never give up on me. I cannot say I have the same state of mind. It has to be you that goes, or I'm afraid our brothers and sisters will be lost to darkness forever." Her eyes darkened with remorse.

"How will I know you will remember us? How can you be sure our love won't die along with my light?" Incaendiel was against the idea from the start. "How do you know you won't die with my light? There are so many things that we aren't sure of, and you just want me jumping with the rest of them." He peered into her eyes. "I could never lose you, Sophie. It would be the end of me. I would strip myself of my grace."

"You have to trust me. My memories will come back from time to time. When it is the final year of my incarnation and time for us to return, I will regain all my memories. Please be patient with me. In the beginning, there will be false memories. I will come around to the light, I promise, as long as you are there by me to guide me." The other angels were lining the edge of the summit to take the plunge. She grabbed him tight and kissed his cheek. "You will never lose me," she whispered into his ear. She felt a tear drop onto her face. "Go, Incaendiel! Go!"

He ran from her and jumped as the last angel. She watched his plunge along with everyone else's. It nearly ripped her own light from her body when he lost his. An angel stood at her side, watching alongside her. She recognized him immediately. Lucifer leaned closer to her and whispered into her ear, "He will never return, and your light will eventually die, but unlike the other angels who are stripped of their light, you will die along with your light."

I awoke gasping for air. Azazel sat forward in her chair. "What!? What is it?" I could see she was alarmed.

"I had a dream," I whispered, gasping in the air.

"Was it a dream, or..." Azazel stopped and studied me. "You had a memory."

I nodded and burst into tears. "It's not going to work. Neither one of us can be saved."

"I don't understand." Azazel stood, walked to the side of my bed, and sat down. "Tell me the memory." So, I sat and went over every detail with her. I hesitated when I got to Lucifer. "What? Tell me."

"He...he told me he would never return." Azazel's eyes grew wide. "And..." I stopped.

"And what!" She was up, pacing the floor, drinking in what I had already told her.

"He said when he didn't return, my light would die." She stopped dead in her tracks.

"No angel's light has ever died!" I stared at her. "Did he say what would happen to you?"

I nodded my head. "He said I would die when his light went out." She stopped dead in her tracks.

Darkness would take over Isaiah, and I would die unless he could fight the darkness and join us in the summit.

"What if I were to stay behind with him in the darkness? Would I die then?" She closed her eyes, and when she opened them back up, tears were in her eyes. The answer was yes. "It's because I'm not a fallen angel, isn't it? You all fell and lost your light. Mine is being sucked away through the darkness of him." I choked back the tears on the last sentence.

Sam appeared next to Azazel and looked between the two of us. "What happened? What did she remember?"

Azazel swallowed, "We need to talk together as a

family."

"Is it that bad?" He stared into Azazel's eyes and could nearly see the full story. "We will go at once." He walked over and took my hand. "All of us."

Within the blink of an eye, we were standing at the base of an ancient mountain. He let my hand down and raised his own hands to the sky. Azazel raised her hands as well, and the ground began to tremble. I thought the mountain was going to split in half. Within a split second, millions of the fallen ones, as far as the eye could see, stood around me.

"Samael, what takes precedence that you would bring her here and summon all of us?" It was the Dark Mother. What was it Gramms called her? Lilith, maybe. She appeared from inside the cave and stood before the three of us.

Sam bowed before her. "Mother, we have troubling news." Her eyes searched the crowd around her.

"Incaendiel?" she asked.

"Is fine for the time being, but what lies ahead for Sophie and him looks grim."

Sam glanced at me. I could see the sorrow in his eyes. Not only had we spent the last ten years growing up together, but we also had centuries together.

"Please enlighten us all, Sophie." She looked at me as if she were peering through me.

"It all started with the dream I had," I told them

the entire memory, including Lucifer. When I finished, there was a hushed silence followed by a tidal wave of yelling.

Lilith held up her hand, and the crowd hushed immediately. "And you are sure those are his exact words to you?" I nodded. "Well, we are in quite a predicament here, are we not?" She turned towards Sam and said, "When the portal opens, he is the only one who can control it. We have to make sure that the last person that goes through grabs his hand before he lets it go."

"Aren't we going to tell him what is fated in the future?" I asked, and everyone turned to look at me. "I received the memory for a reason. In the entire eighteen years I have been alive, I have never dreamt before. Someone sent me that memory on purpose. We must warn him!" I was desperate, looking from Lilith to Sam.

"Who do you think sent you the memory?" Lilith walked over and lifted my face to her eyes. She frightened and comforted me all at once. It was an odd sensation.

"I believe it was Lucifer. No one else would have known that memory." Lilith studied my face closer and closer.

"I believe you are right. It has been some time now, and Lucifer was to have already joined our ranks. I suppose Alpha's punishment to him carried more severity than I thought it would have. Undoubtedly, he is free and ready to join us, or he would not have sent us the message. Let us prepare for his arrival." She sauntered back into the cave entrance while Sam and Azazel led me down as well. My eyes searched the crowd of angels for Isaiah, but he wasn't here.

As if answering the question that came to my mind, Azazel said, "He's not here. Sam didn't call him. He left him to meditate at the lake."

My eyes dropped to the ground in shame. It was my words that caused his out-of-control behavior.

"It wasn't your fault, Sister; it was Father's."

I watched her catch up to Sam's pace. It dawned on me. These are angels, fallen or not, and unlike humans who blame God for everything, for once, the blame was proportioned correctly. It was entirely his fault, all this.

As we took the last few steps, everyone froze in place. I didn't know if they were going to attack or run from what they saw. I inched closer to the edge of the crowd and peered in between Sam and Azazel. In the middle of the room stood Lilith, and beside her stood an enormous angel with black wings. When I looked closer at him, his skin was the same color as the others, so he was a fallen one. *Which angel had chosen to fall? I thought they all fell at one time. Were there other fallen angels that were new since the big fall?* When his eyes met mine and I saw his face, I knew exactly who it was.

    "Lucifer."

CHAPTER 9

The Pain of Memory Gained

"THE MEMORY of a life before can stand the test of time. Even locked away from the soul's undying light can never make the memory drown. The pain of memories will hurt for a while, and in due time go away. What is important is the memory itself and that it never ever fades away."

"SOPHIE, it's nice to see you. God, I've missed you." He walked over and gave me a huge hug. When he pulled me back, he could see the confusion written in my eyes. "Well, I see not all your memories have returned."

"What do you mean by that?" I asked, eyeing him. "Were you the one who sent the dream to me?"

"Yes, it was me. You needed a push back into the direction you were supposed to go. The memory I returned to you was the one our father had me pluck from your mind. He wanted the last few moments you had with Incaendiel before he fell. Of course, I couldn't tell him no. I could only obey. So, I hid your memory, awaiting my release from the tower to return it to you." *The tower? What the hell is the tower?* He could see the questions mounting on my face. "The tower is where the angels are sent for punishment. There is no light, no visitors, only time to think and ponder on what you have done to disgrace yourself. I'm surprised you don't remember it, considering every nineteen years you are imprisoned there away from all the other angels awaiting your next incarnation."

"He locks me away? Why?!" I was hurt and furious. The father in the Bible is nowhere near comparable to the evil of the true father.

"So, you won't lead any more angels astray." He snickered at me and winked.

I could feel my cheeks burn. He wasn't that bad-looking, and no one had ever paid me this much attention while growing up. My eyes danced around wildly between all the faces.

"Sorry it took me so long, Mother. My punishment earned more time than I had planned with the stunt I pulled in Jerusalem." He chuckled.

"Ah, yes, what was it that you called out to your father?" Lilith smiled.

"Why has thou forsaken me," I replied. They all looked at me, stunned. "What? It's in the King James Bible. Everyone knows that line."

"What else is in the Bible that Alpha saw to being made?" Lilith asked.

"There's lots in the Bible. It spoke of the creation story, but far from the one in Gramms' Bible. It did have you sneaking back into the Garden and whispering to Eve to eat the fruit. Wise move on your part. There was the flood with Noah's ark, Lott, and the city of Sodom and Gomorra. Oh, there is also an entire book in itself for Lucifer." I looked over at him. "Did you really go by the name of Jesus Christ?"

"Who knows, maybe that will surface in a memory." He winked at me again. "What story does it tell about me?" He was truly intrigued by having a book of his own.

"It has bits and pieces of your life up until 12 years old, where they lost you at the temple. From there to around 30 to 33 years old, your life was erased. There

121

was nothing until John the Baptist baptized you." I looked at him while he was snickering. "What's so funny?"

"Did the book say I told my parents they should have known I would be in the house of my father?" I looked at him quizzically.

"Yea. I don't get the joke." I looked at the few angels who were beginning to snicker along with him. "What's funny about that?"

"It's a bit of sarcasm. If you remembered what His house did look like, you would laugh at it being compared to a temple. It's an insult on his behalf. I got a couple of floggings for that comment." He chuckled again and reminisced on all the sarcasm he threw at Alpha while he was a mortal.

"What news do you bring from the summit, Lucifer?" It was Samael who asked.

"Everyone is pretty pissed that Sophie remembered Incaendiel. Father told them she would never remember him, and you all would stay as fallen angels. Father also has them convinced that being away from your light for so long has turned you into vile creatures that he likes to call Demons. On another note, Michael has been unusually quiet, especially with that last encounter with Incaendiel here at the entrance to the Glade."

"When did that happen? He didn't report that to me?" Sam asked with a hint of anger on his words.

"It was the day of the party, is all I know. Ask a few of the brothers here. It seemed as if he called them forth as a first in command could." I don't know if Lucifer was taunting Sam or not, but Sam was furious.

"I was told I alone had that power. How is it he can call them forth too, Mother!" He was pacing with fury.

"Calm down, Samael. He doesn't want your position in the infantry. He was surrounded by ten of your summit brothers and felt like he needed assistance." Lilith placed her hand on his shoulder to calm him.

"How does he hold that power without the rank?" I was wondering the same thing as well as everyone gathered around.

"I have kept Incaendiel's power from all of you. His power is far greater in strength, and it uses less of his grace to accomplish. His emotions trigger the most hazardous moments for those who stand around." She looked at me as she said that sentence. My mind flashed back to the burning lake, and a shiver went through me.

"He has known for quite some time about his power over all of you, but all he wishes is to get you home safe and sound and back to your light." She sighed. "Incaendiel's power is what is causing the darkness to seek him out. It wants his power to be used for evil. He has fought this darkness for centuries. If it does not work this time, he will be overcome with the darkness, and we will never reach the summit." Everyone fell silent.

I looked at Lucifer, who returned my look. He will never return echoed in my mind.

"No! This time, we all go home. There won't be a next time." Everyone's eyes fell on me. "How do I remember where the Garden is?" No one answered me. "How?!" I demanded. I couldn't let Isaiah be consumed by darkness all because of me.

The voice that echoed through the Glade was one I did not expect. "You are the Garden. The garden lies within your light." Isaiah stood at the back of the room.

Everyone parted as he made his way to the front of the room. He stood before me without reaching out to me.

"It's nice to see you again, Lucifer. Sorry, I couldn't make it to Jerusalem. You know how much I detest brutality against mankind."

"No problem, Brother. It's good to see you too." He walked over and threw his arms around Incaendiel. "From what I hear, you live up to the name you were given, you little pyro."

He noogied his head, and Incaendiel grinned; they looked as if they had truly grown up as great friends. I don't think I could ever get used to calling him anything aside from Isaiah.

"So how do we get the Garden to spring forth from my light?" I asked, walking over to him.

"The same way Mother and Father created it." He paused, brushing a strand of hair behind my ear.

"How was that?" I asked in barely a whisper.

"Through love," Lilith replied.

"I don't understand. I already love him; shouldn't that be enough?" I was confused by her reply. I loved him; I did.

"You have to surrender yourself completely to him just as things were before. You two must become as One, and the enchantment will break." I understood completely what she meant that time. I flashed back into the car with Dean and shivered.

"Is that why...Dean..."

"Yes." Incaendiel cut me off before I could finish the sentence. His eyes flashed with anger when I mentioned his name.

"Keep your emotions under control, my son, or you will set us all ablaze." Lilith put her hand on his shoulder, but I could still see the tension in his body language.

"It doesn't have to be right now...does it? I mean, as an eighteen-year-old girl, I don't know if I'm ready for...that." I swallowed hard. This was a conversation meant for private, not to be out in the open in front of everyone. Isaiah smiled at me.

"We have until 11:59 the night before your birthday." I nodded. My face flushed, and I quickly changed the subject.

"Am I still in danger from the others?" Once more, I watched Isaiah tense up.

"No, neither of you is free from the wrath of the others." It was Lucifer who spoke this time. "Before I fell, I heard them conspiring a kidnapping. I couldn't tell who it was they proposed to take. It's one reason I took the plunge. That way, you would be prepared for it. The best thing for both of you right now is to stay together and guarded by at least two at all times."

"I agree. Sam and Azazel have made this small town their home alongside Incaendiel. I think it's best that they stay their guards." Lilith spoke and turned to Lucifer. "And maybe a surprise one."

"Whatever is needed, mother." He bowed to her. There was a tremendous rumble, and it sounded like lightning struck the mountain and nearly toppled it.

Lilith turned to Lucifer. "Were you expecting company to join?"

"No, I was not," he said, disappearing in a flash. Incaendiel grabbed my hand, and in a zap, we were at the base of the mountain. Everyone stood around a crater in the ground. When the floating dirt and debris settled, everyone peered at who stepped out of the hole and gasped.

"Michael?" Incaendiel was astonished.

"Now, Brother, that I have your trust, do you

mind telling me how we're all getting our light restored." He looked between Isaiah and me.

"Is there anyone else abandoning Alpha and planning to join?" Lilith asked.

Michael teared up and ran to her, throwing his arms around her.

"Mother, how I have missed your face."

It seemed like he wept for hours holding her when he pulled away. I had never known that Michael could be such a softie with his legends of war and his sword of wrath.

"Metatron is on the ropes, but I'm sure he will join as well. All of us dearly miss you." He looked around at all the fallen ones. "We have missed you all. We want you to return home!" The tears glistened in his eyes.

"And this isn't a trick of Father's, sending a spy down to see how close we are to returning?" Incaendiel said with more malice than he intended.

"Do you think I would have given up my light to spy on you?" Michael glared at Incaendiel.

"You have proven to be a trickster before. What's to stop you now? I'm sure you weren't just 'summoned' away, leaving Zadkiel behind." Incaendiel stepped forth as if challenging Michael.

"What he speaks is the truth," Lucifer stated. "No one can lie in my presence, or have you forgotten the gift bestowed upon me, Brother?"

I touched his arm and had him look me in my

eyes. "I believe him, Incaendiel." Practice makes perfect. He seemed to melt before my eyes as I said his true name.

No sooner had I said it than there were streaks of light falling through the sky. It looked like shooting stars falling and impacting the Earth. It truly makes you wonder if the streaks in the sky at night are meteors or angels dancing around. The ground shook and trembled to where I could barely stand on my feet. Incaendiel grabbed me by my waist to steady me. A mass of angels walked forth. The one in front was astonishingly perfect in every way. He was toned in the spots he needed to be and muscled in the others. He looked like a Greek God stepping out of a movie.

"It's nice to see you, Metatron." Lucifer walked over and hugged his brother.

"Well, when Michael left, we noted his seriousness. There have been many talks over who would help and who wouldn't. Not to mention our conversations we've held in private. This cause must be far greater than the one Father has in store for us all." His gaze slipped over to mine, and his eyes twinkled. "It's nice to see you again, Sophie. It has been far too long that Father has kept you all to himself."

I shuddered at those words. If he meant keeping me locked away, as Lucifer had said, I can't see how that was keeping me to himself. He looked over at Incaendiel and bowed.

"What are the orders, Brother?"

I heard Sam grunt behind me and mutter something under his breath.

"I am not first in command. Orders come from Samael, not me," Incaendiel said as he stepped aside and bowed to Sam. Sam's angry face melted away, and for once, I saw him smile at Incaendiel.

Just thinking his name sent ripples throughout my body. I saw he had the same effect when I thought his name as goosebumps prickled on his arms. What astonished me, even more, was the voice I heard back in my head.

"It does me too."

I looked at him; he smiled and winked at me. Each day was more of a surprise with him and the bond we share.

"Have we always been like this?" I thought directly to him.

"Yes," he replied.

"Ah, realizing you two have telecommunication for the first time. It's so cute!" Lucifer flapped his hand in front of his face as if he were going to cry like a chick in a movie. "I'm so proud of my babies." He pretended like he was going to cry, covering his mouth with the tips of his fingers.

We laughed at him. I see why everyone liked him. I wish I could have known him as Jesus. I heard a giggle in my head.

"That was funny!" I nearly laughed out loud.

"Now, now, you two. It's not polite to telecommunicate about people behind their backs," Lucifer chided.

Metatron turned his attention to Lilith. "So now what, Mother? I'm surprised Father hasn't had a tantrum yet finding out his best angels fell from the light."

As if to prove his point, a lightning storm ensued. A bolt dropped right in front of Incaendiel and me. We both jumped back, and his hand gripped mine, preparing to bolt to safety.

"Well, Metatron, I think he just realized." Lilith laughed and pushed the lightning storm away from the mountain with her hand. "First thing's first, we need to devise a protection team for Incaendiel and Sophie. With Alpha losing some of his top-notch angels, he will be more devious than before. The plan we had earlier needs to be reinforced. Samael and Azazel, you will keep your detail as close as possible to the two of them." They nodded in agreement. "Lucifer, I want you at least within a mile radius of those two in case they need your assistance." He nodded in agreeance. "Metatron and Michael, I want you two to keep your radius within the bounds of the town. Alpha only knows who will be sent next to strike, and they need to be thoroughly protected."

She looked over at Sam and Azazel. "You two need to drop the human bodies and take back your angelic forms. You are more susceptible than humans. You can cast a glamor over your wings so no one will see them. Incaendiel has to remain human until the last moment as it is, I don't need you two to be in the same amount of danger."

"Why would he be in danger?" I asked.

All eyes trained on me.

"Angels in human form are not impervious to death. I'm surprised your last incarnation on Earth hasn't surfaced as a memory yet. It would show you better than what I could tell you." She looked over at Incaendiel, worried. "In order for the Garden to surface correctly through her, she has to have all her memories, or it won't work."

"If I'm not mistaken, Father has her memories locked away from her. Someone will have to retrieve them for her to remember," Lucifer said as he walked over to me. He looked me in my eyes, peering deeply within. "They do not exist in her mind."

"How are we going to do this then?" Samael blurted out.

"Everyone, relax. I told you I wouldn't fall from the light without having a purpose," Michael stated.

He reached into the bag he was carrying and retrieved a jar full of glowing white balls. They looked beautiful.

"I do believe these will help in our crusade." He

smiled as he handed them over to Incaendiel.

"It looks like you two have some work ahead. Remember, do not give her more than three memories at a time, or you will cause her brain to hemorrhage. These are angelic memories, not human ones." Lilith looked to us both to ensure we understood. We both nodded.

"So, where are we headed?" Sam asked, stepping forth.

Azazel was at his side. I believe there was more than just brother and sister between the two of them, but I knew it was rude to ask. Maybe it will be in one of my memories.

"The lake. It seems to be the perfect spot for her memories to come forth." Incaendiel smiled down at me.

I returned the smile faintly. I remembered what the lake looked like before we left, and I wasn't sure I wanted to return to that spot.

He bent down and whispered in my ear, "Don't worry. It looks like it did when we first went there." He scooped me up in his arms and took off into the night sky.

We landed at the lake, and he was right. It looked exactly the way it did the first time we went there. Sam and Azazel took posts on opposite sides of the lake. Incaendiel disappeared for a moment, then reappeared with my comforter and laid it down on the ground. He motioned for me to sit, and he took a seat beside me. The close proximity to him sent ripples through my body. I fought back the urge to climb in his lap. A smile formed on his lips, making me blush. He knew what I wanted.

"Not right now. We must get a few memories in first. This jar is slammed full of centuries of memories. It may take the entire year to return them to you. Are you ready?" He turned to me, looking nervously.

I stared at him. Millions of questions ran through my head. "How did you nearly die last time? I want to be told before I remember."

He sighed. "I was afraid you would ask me. It's better if you remember than me telling you."

"Please, just tell me a little?" My eyes pleaded with his.

He hesitated before he spoke. "I was protecting you." Of course, he was. "We all assumed the reason you died on your nineteenth birthday was so Alpha could lock you away. Lucifer confirmed it. I hated the thought of you being locked away from me."

He tensed up. I could feel the anger radiating through him.

"You know you have to love Alpha no matter what, right? It's the only way you can receive your light again."

I watched as a tear slid down his cheek. I wiped it from his face, and he looked over at me.

"I will always love my father. That doesn't mean I will see eye to eye on what he does." He opened the jar and reached in for a memory. "Are you ready?"

I breathed in deep. I wasn't sure if I was ready, but it was the only way for all of us to return to the light. I knew he couldn't last another one thousand years without the light. I had no choice.

"I'm ready. How does this work? Do I eat the ball or what?" He smiled.

He bent down and kissed my lips. My heart skipped a beat, and I felt the heat rush through my body. Before I knew it, I was spiraling down a black hole.

CHAPTER 10

The Garden of Good and Evil

"WALK WITH ME MA' Lady through the garden of chaos and havoc. As your demon of redemption holds your heart, the angel of salvation holds your hand. What is salvation and what is redemption in your mind's eye? Can it be your angel is the devil and your demon is the one that flies in the light?"

WHEN THE HAZE DISAPPEARED, I was in a medieval-type dress. *How did I change clothes, especially into ones that are, shall I say, out of season?* I sat up from the bed I was lying in and noticed the lake had disappeared from around me. From that moment forth, everything was on autopilot. I could think for myself, but the words I would say were from the memory.

I walked to the window and peered out of the gaping hole. I lived in a castle. There were banners and streamers everywhere. The servants dashed around the courtyard, assembling everything for a celebration. *What day is it?* There was a knock at the door, and I left my post at the window.

"You may enter." Wow, me speaking proper and all. The person who walked through the door froze my heart. It was Dean. I wanted to shout at him to leave, to ask what he was doing here. Instead, I said, "Dean, what a pleasant surprise. Pray, tell me, why do you call on me?" He walked over to me and took my hand. He bent down and kissed it. "Such a modest gentleman."

"Ma' Lady, you look stunning. Would you accompany me to breakfast in the grand hall? The king and queen request your attendance for formal announcements of your birthday celebration in a few days." He smiled an earnest smile at me.

I wanted to refuse, but instead, my body replied, "Of course, lead the way, good sir." I roped my arm through his, and he escorted me to the grand hall.

We settled into our seats to the left of my mother. I looked around at the grand assemblage of people. It seemed as if kingdoms from around the world had made their way for the celebration of my birthday. *Which birthday is this, my eighteenth or my nineteenth?* The servants began serving everyone their food. My plate was stacked full of every type of food imaginable. I couldn't eat all that, and my body agreed as I nibbled on the food.

The king, my father, stood to make his announcement. "I would like to thank all of you for assembling for the celebration of my daughter Sophie's nineteenth birthday. Two moons from now, we will celebrate both her birthday and her engagement to my future heir, Dean, Prince of Eden."

My mouth nearly dropped open. *Engagement! Was he serious? I didn't want to marry this piece of crap!* My face betrayed my mind, and I smiled as the applause went through the air. He took my hand and kissed it once more. I cringed inwardly. *This was so wrong. Where was Incaendiel? Have I pushed him completely away?* Just as if it were on cue, Incaendiel made his way to our table. He was dressed as one of the servants. He looked directly into my eyes, and my heart fluttered. This was a real reaction as I felt Dean tense beside me. I could feel the sparks between us as we gazed at each other.

"More wine, Ma 'Lady?" He held up the wine pitcher, and I nodded. He topped off my glass of wine and turned to Dean. "More wine, good sir?"

Dean scowled at him and flicked him away with his hand. I watched him proceed with the queen and king next. Once he was finished serving the royal table, he returned the same way he had come and smiled at me.

"The first thing I will do as heir to the throne is send that servant boy to the gallows." I tensed up after Dean said that.

"You will do no such thing!" I said it a bit louder than I had intended.

My mother cleared her throat, motioning me to lower my tone in front of the men. I glared over at Dean,

"If you harm him in any way, I will call the wedding off and have you sent to the gallows for treason. Do not forget, I know the real reason you seek my hand in marriage. Just know it will not work. You can try all you want, but it will never work!" I hissed under my breath. "Mother, Father, is my attendance still required at this moment? I feel a bit flushed and need a walk through the garden to cool off."

"Very well, Sophie. If you feel ill, let a servant know. Don't pass out in the rose bushes again."

Mother was a bit cheeky with her last statement, but I ignored it. It wasn't rude for the princess to excuse herself from the table, but a guest of honor sitting there had to remain there through the entire feast, which could last for hours.

I snaked my way through the empty castle corridors until my feet hit the grass of the garden. I removed my shoes and sat them at the door. I stepped through the door and out into the garden. I immediately felt the warmth of the sun wash over me. I closed my eyes and drank in the warmth. When I opened my eyes, Incaendiel stood before me. I grinned ear to ear.

"I was hoping you would follow me."

"The queen felt as if an escort would be proper considering your last faint in the roses." He smiled at me, and my heart somersaulted.

"My birthday is in two moons, are you going to attend the celebrations as well?" His smile turned into a frown.

"You know I cannot, Sophie."

He looked so sad. I wanted to profess my love to him but was unable to. Apparently, this Sophie loved him but didn't admit it to him. I reminded myself that in this lifetime, Dean had his hooks in me until the last moment. I couldn't help but stare at him. I knew he was my love. Something tugged at the edge of my mind, something evil and foreboding. A memory hit me hard, a memory from this time period. My brain felt as if it was going to bust as it surfaced.

"I told you not to consort with him. He is the Devil in the flesh. He is here to turn you to the dark side!" Dean hissed at me.

I stared off after Incaendiel as he left the corridor we had been standing in. This was nearly a year before now. My heart would beat faster around him than I had ever experienced.

"Then maybe I am a child of darkness as well," I replied.

He grabbed me by my hand and whipped me around to look at his face.

"You are not of the dark! You are a child of the light! Remember that!" He threw my hand back down to my side and breathed in a deep breath. "This is important, Sophie. He will lead you down the wrong path. He will draw you into the darkness, and the Lord will not forgive for that!" He towed me down the hall back to my chamber room and bid me goodnight.

I snapped back from the interlude and grabbed my head. Incaendiel grabbed me before I hit the ground. "Are you okay?"

His eyes searched mine. They were so sincere in their concern. *How could he be evil?* He was far more angelic than what Dean was.

"I'm fine. It's just Dean trying to get into my head."

He tensed when I said Dean's name, and I could sense his jealousy over him. It felt nice to have a quarrel over my hand. Before Dean came along, no others had voiced interest in me.

"Sophie, you realize this is more important than just gaining your hand in marriage." He was always so serious.

"Yes, I understand that the cosmos are out of balance, and you want to get back into heaven. I know!" He always found a way to irritate me and break me from the bliss I sank into whenever he was around.

"Do you?"

He stopped and turned to look in my eyes. I guess my eyes told him what he didn't want to hear.

"Just don't let him get too close. He's deceiving you to get what he wants, not what's best for you." He left. He left me standing out in the garden just as the rain started to roll in. I remember feeling the pain shoot through my heart. I hated it when he would leave me alone. I had always felt like a piece of myself was missing. This must have been the part of myself that absolutely loved him trying to break through to the surface.

The memory flashed forward to the night before my nineteenth birthday. Dean was escorting me to some play that he had reserved tickets for. We took the horse and carriage out of the castle. We traveled for what seemed like hours when it should have only been an hour's way out.

"Dean, where are we going? We are far out from the city where the play should have been."

I looked at him in the light from the lantern. His face was blank and sinister. From how dreadfully dark it had become, I could only imagine how late at night it could be.

"Mother and Father will disapprove of me being out so late."

He finally looked over at me, but the look in his eyes was more frightening to me as opposed to the lashing I would get being out so late with a man.

"Tonight is the final night, Sophie. You will give me what I came for. I have been patiently playing with you for a year now. I always get what I want." He sneered at me in the dark.

My heart raced with fear and panic. I thought I would pass out from the sheer fright he gave me.

"Dean, turn this carriage around and take me home!" I tried to sound harsh, but I know it came out meek and as a whisper.

"You will do as I say, Princess!"

His words filled me with a feeling I had never felt before. Terror ripped through my body as I made a break for the carriage door, but he grabbed me by the waist and held me down on the floor.

"Where is the Garden?"

His voice sent dread through my body. It was no longer compassionate or angelic. It was dark and eerie.

"I-I don't know where the Garden is! I swear!"

No matter how much I struggled, he was ten times stronger than me and had no problem holding me down.

"You will tell me where it is if I have to beat it from your dead body!"

He was more than terrifying at this moment. I knew deep down he wasn't lying about what he would do.

"I don't know where it is! I can't tell you something I don't know!" I glanced around the carriage, but there was nothing I could use as a weapon.

"We have but a few minutes until it is 12 at night. You have to tell me where it is or suffer a death you have never imagined before."

It was almost as if his voice pleaded with mine. Tears streamed from my eyes. I knew I was going to die tonight. I didn't know where the Garden everyone asked me about existed. I had never been there; how was I to know where it was? It existed

143

millenniums ago when God created the world. I wasn't there!

"Dean, please, I don't know where it is! Please, let me go! I want to go home! Please, just let me go home!" I pleaded with him.

His eyes looked like they softened to my plea.

"You want to go home?" He asked with such sincerity that I genuinely believed he was going to take me home.

"Yes," I whispered through tears.

"I'm sorry, Sophie. You're going home, not just the one here on Earth."

He put his hands around my throat and began choking me. I couldn't get a breath in to scream for help. Tiny dots started floating in my vision, and I went down a tunnel. *This was it. He's going to choke me to death! How I wished I had listened to Incaendiel. Where is my knight when I need him?* As the dark started to swallow me, I threw out the last plea I had, which was really a reconciliation of my heart. *I love you, Incaendiel!* I felt the weight of Dean pulled off of me. I choked and gasped for air. No relief came to my lungs. I lay there gasping for air, but not a single gasp let air in. He must have crushed my windpipe. Images blurred in and out in front of my face. I saw Incaendiel lean over the top of me. There was blood on his shirt and on his hands.

I could hear through a tunnel a whispered voice, "Sophie, Sophie, come back to me." A hazy heat engulfed me as I realized the carriage was on fire.

"Go!" I choked out in a raspy voice that could have only been a whisper.

The world was caving in on itself around me. He didn't move. I could see the fire start to burn his clothes. As my vision went black, I saw a set of hands pull him from the carriage, and then there was nothing.

CHAPTER 11

S aving Grace

"ONCE UPON A MIDNIGHT BLUE, I sat and gazed at a world untrue. Through mine eyes and through his soul, I saw the story of the world unfold. Tears of strength and pain seep down, as the memory of the flesh is sound. And as my eyelids flutter open from fear, the arms of assurance surely are here. Swiftly we will be pulled from one another, as dawn emerges with wings a flutter."

I AWOKE, choking and screaming. I gasped for air, fearing that the memory had turned into a real consequence. Tears were streaming down my face, and I realized Incaendiel had been holding me. I turned and cried into his chest. I heaved the tears out, trying to find my voice.

"It was horrible! I don't want to see any others! Please don't make me relive any more of them." I cried, and he rocked me in his arms. "How could I have been so stupid to trust him! I didn't think angels were allowed to murder humans. It goes against their nature!"

I could still feel Dean's hands around my throat. It explained his nature to me when he first came back, why he was so indignant. My head thumped tremendously, like someone had dropped an anvil on it. Incaendiel didn't move. He just sat there and held me until I had cried the entire memory out into his shirt.

"Please, Incaendiel, please don't make me see another one."

I could feel him swallow hard. I knew he didn't want me to suffer anymore, but there was no choice.

"Sophie." He was choking back tears. "Please stop begging me not to do what you know we have to." His voice quivered, and I knew it was from him choking back the emotions welling.

Everything I felt, I knew he felt as well. Everything I thought, I already knew he thought. So,

147

everything I experienced in my memory, he did as well.

I felt slightly dizzy and out of sorts.

"Do we have to do them back-to-back, or can I get a break in between them? My head really hurts."

He stroked my hair and wiped the tears from my face.

"Of course, we can wait in between them. I had Lucifer bring you some food. You need to eat in between the memories."

He sat me up and motioned over to the food and drink setting there. The sun was just peeking above the horizon. I had forgotten it was nighttime when we had come out here. Waking up in the darkness must have triggered a real-life panic attack as I felt my breathing going back to normal. The food came into my view, and I could smell fresh pancakes and coffee. It turns out Lucifer had gone to a late-night breakfast joint and got takeout for two. We both sat there, silently eating and drinking the coffee. As the sun peaked higher above the horizon, it cast enough light onto Incaendiel that I could see his face. He was a wreck. I could only imagine what I looked like.

"So, you felt everything I did as though you were experiencing it." I looked over at him, and he flinched.

"It's not the first time I felt it. I should have followed you two once you left the castle. I was given orders not to. I never forgot what happened that night. When he showed up with you at the rec center, I wanted to choke the life from his body. If Samael and Rafe hadn't been there, I would have. He was dangling his stake on you once more in front of me, and I could do nothing about it."

He swallowed a drink of coffee, and I watched as he fought back the anger building from thinking about Dean.

"How many times have you tried to save me from dying?" I regretted asking as soon as I did.

He nearly choked on his food. He was silent as if battling whether he should tell me or not.

"I've never gotten as close to saving you as I did last time. Mother was not happy that I intervened at all, especially since I nearly died with you in the fire." His face took on a dark shadow.

"You know it wasn't the fire that killed me, right?" I asked, looking over at him.

He just turned away from me.

"I know. That bastard choked the life from you. He wasn't even punished for it. Mother was furious. I swore if I ever had the chance to get even with him over it, I would."

I reached over and touched his hand. The electricity calmed my heart. He was taking in deep breaths. I knew the anger was still fresh from the ordeal. I understood why he was so angry to have seen Dean show up at the field the day I drove him there. If it hadn't been for Sam making him walk away, he really would have killed Dean.

"Incaendiel?"

He looked over at me, and just hearing his name, he melted into my eyes. He leaned in and kissed me. The heat coursed through my body. I pulled away, though, fearful he was going to thrust another memory into me.

His voice came to me in my head, "It's okay. I just want to feel you in my arms. You're not ready for another memory."

I let him pull me back in and kiss me. The power between us surged through my veins. I could feel my heart beating and thought it would explode out of my chest. This feeling I had never experienced. I was eighteen and had never kissed a boy before him.

"Did you stake a claim on me at school? Is that why I was never asked out on dates?" I heard him chuckle and groan over the question.

"Do you really think I would let someone weasel you away from me? You were mine." I could feel the smile from the words as he wrapped his arms tighter around me.

"I love you."

It kind of slipped out in our silent thoughts. He immediately pulled away. I was confused as to why he pulled away after I told him I loved him. It felt like a knife stabbed me in the heart. I was pouring my heart out to him in every way I thought possible.

"What's wrong?" I asked. He didn't reply to me. "Incaendiel?"

He got up from where he was sitting and walked to the edge of the lake. Lucifer dropped in right after he got up. He looked me over, and the look in his eyes was all I needed to confirm I looked like crap.

"So, I can see the memory was hard on you." He sat down beside me. "That was the worst one because it was the most recent." He glanced over to Incaendiel. "Not to mention, it was the most horrific. Father found it funny that Dean took your life into his own hands. He promoted him for the deed. A lot of us angels objected, but he threatened us with the tower to keep quiet."

Lucifer looked down as he sat with his legs drawn up but apart. He could pass as a regular human in his mannerisms. Then again, at one point, he had been human.

"Not that it mattered to me since I was already locked away."

He looked over at me as I sat silently watching Incaendiel. He touched my hand, so I would glance up at him.

"What's wrong, angel?"

I knew I was an angel, but the way he said it tugged at something that I couldn't grasp. I shook the feeling off.

"I did something that upset him," I said, sipping

my coffee and setting it back down.

"Was it during your head chats?" *Wow, he was rather good at knowing things.* "It's a gift." He laughed.

"Touché." I chuckled back.

My eyes trailed over to Incaendiel. He just sat there staring off into the water. I heard Lucifer sigh beside me.

"What?" I asked, returning my attention to him.

"It's not my place to tell you." He followed my gaze over to Incaendiel.

"Tell me what?" He had piqued my interest.

"What is it that you tell him in your mind but never out loud?"

I was confused. Most of the things I told him in my mind, he already knew because he was reading it.

"I will give you another hint. What was the plea you called out to him your last incarnation before you died?"

I thought for a moment, not really wanting to recall the choking part. "I told him I love you." I glanced over at him, but he was ignoring our conversation.

"He can't hear us talking, another gift of mine." He smiled at me. "Have you ever told him out loud how you feel?"

"He knows how I feel. He reads my mind and can feel it from my emotions." *That couldn't be the reason why, could it?*

"But have you ever out loud told him I love you."

I thought back to the moment at the lake. I could have sworn I told him then, but I didn't. I only kissed him, showing him how I felt. It sank in.

"No, I haven't." My eyes dropped to the ground, and my face reddened.

"You will when the moment is right. He must realize that it's a different lifetime and that you need time to say it out loud. It has been quite some time since you two spoke openly about how you felt with one another."

He stood up and looked over at Incaendiel. He was still sitting at the edge of the lake.

"I'm going to go scope the area again. I hope you enjoyed the breakfast."

I nodded, and he smiled, pleased. His eyes lingered on me for a moment, and I watched him fly off. I returned my attention back to Incaendiel. *Is that what he really needed? Did he need to hear the human me tell him how much my soul loves him?*

I stood from my seat, a bit shaky, but I stretched it out. I walked over to the edge of the lake and sat down beside him. He didn't look at me. I touched his hand, but he tucked it away from me. Even though I wanted to tell him, I was nervous as hell to try and say it out loud.

"Incaendiel?"

He didn't look at me; apparently, that doesn't

have the same effect on him anymore. I scooted over and plopped myself down in his lap so he would have to look at me.

"Will you please look at me or acknowledge me?"

It took him a moment, but his eyes finally met mine. They were so gray and dismal. The vibrant blue they had been was now dim. I searched in his eyes for a sign of life. He was shut down. I leaned forward and kissed his lips, but he didn't return the gesture. I kissed his cheek, then his forehead. I kissed his chin and then his jaw. I made my way down to his neck and kissed it. I could feel him shiver beneath me. I placed my hands on his face and made him look me in the eyes. His eyes looked so lost, so empty. It was my turn to save him. "I-"

"Incoming!" is all I heard.

I didn't even get to finish my sentence when he picked me up from his lap and sat me down on the ground. He made a dash for the jar, screwed the lid on it, and blinked it away. The sky was littered with angels. My heart dropped to my feet when I saw Dean in front of them all. Sam and Azazel were at my side like a blur. Incaendiel stood in front of us, looking at the army that came for us.

"Well, well, isn't this lovely." Dean smiled that sly grin of his. "So, Sophie, do you remember me now?" My blood ran cold as I flashed back to his hands around my neck, choking the life from me. "Ah, so you do. Hopefully, this time, I can feel your life leave underneath my hands without any interruption." Incaendiel clenched his fists. *Where was Lucifer?* "Waiting for reinforcements? I fear they won't get here in time to help."

He laughed, but it didn't last long as the ground began to quake. I nearly toppled over into the lake, but Azazel grabbed me before I fell in. Lucifer, Metatron, and Michael stood before us alongside Incaendiel.

"There are my fallen brothers. Tell me, how does it feel to lose the light? It must have hurt giving up such an essential part of your being," he snickered.

"It's not the first time I have gone without my light," Lucifer replied coolly.

Dean scowled at him. "Father will love it when I bring you back to him to imprison."

"Are you that daft? You can't bring us back to the summit. In order to cross the threshold, we have to have our light!" Metatron barked.

I could see the entire fleet of angels shiver from the sound of his voice. Even as a fallen angel, they still feared the power the first in command held when he was used to being in charge of them.

"What do you want, Dean?" Michael asked, annoyed.

Even when he was surrounded by the fleet of angels in the sky, he didn't seem too fearful. He had his hand on the hilt of his sword. I guess that's what made him the angel of war and strength.

"A few things, actually. One, Father wants the jar you stole from his cabinet before you fell." Dean glanced around. "I see it has already been hidden." He glared at Incaendiel. "Two, I either want Incaendiel or Sophie. I can either take one of them by force, or you can give one of them up freely."

"Is that all?" Metatron mocked.

"That's not all I want, but what I want doesn't matter to father. Are you going to comply?" He looked between us. Incaendiel backed up and grabbed my hand. "Oh, blinking will be pointless. We have a barrier up; no one gets in, and no one gets out." Panic surged through me. We were trapped with the end result being either Incaendiel or I was going with them.

"Let me go with them." I could feel the anger from him.

"Are you crazy? No! I will not allow it!" Men are always stubborn.

"If they kill me, I will just reincarnate again in one thousand years. If they kill you, you die forever, and they win!" I could still feel his anger, and it was intensifying.

"No! I can handle them."

"Incaendiel, please, just let me do this."

"No." He looked over at Lucifer. "Lucifer, make sure everyone gets in the water and stays under the

156

water." Lucifer glanced over to Incaendiel.

"You can't. They are our brothers!" He was pleading with him.

"I have no choice. If they take either one of us, it's game over forever; we will never see the light again. I can't have that on my shoulders. I will not be the reason why my brothers never returned to the light. At least when you die in battle, you get an honorable burial in the sky. Just do as I ask, please!"

Lucifer couldn't argue. Metatron and Michael had already gotten in the water with Sam and Azazel.

Lucifer looked at me with pain in his eyes. "We have to get in the water." Fear tore through me.

"N-n-no. I-I can't! I can't swim! I panic in the water! Every time, I nearly die from stupidity!" I looked back at the water and could already feel myself drowning. "Please, please, please!" I pleaded, but Lucifer picked me up and carried me out into the water.

It was up to my neck, and I already felt as if the water was rushing into my lungs. Tears of fear were streaming down my face.

"Incaendiel, I can't do this!"

He turned around and looked at me.

"Yes, you can."

He nodded for all of them to go under. I sucked in a breath just in time as Lucifer dove under the water. My heart thudded in my chest, and I immediately felt the need to go up for a breath. Lucifer wouldn't let me move. That's when I felt it, the heat. The water in the lake began to superheat, and I strained through the water to see why. Incaendiel had started a firestorm above the water. If I didn't drown in the water, I was going to boil to death.

If you could cry underwater, you would have seen streams of tears coming from my eyes. I was inconsolable. That was when it happened. I lost all control of my breath and sucked in water. I began struggling in Lucifer's arms. I needed to get to the surface, or I would drown. Apparently, Incaendiel wasn't finished. Lucifer wouldn't let me go. I could feel my lungs slowly fill with the lake water. Everything went hazy in my vision, and I felt myself going down a black tunnel. It was the same black tunnel I had gone through when Dean choked me to death. It was a similar death, but water induced this time. It was funny and ironic to think how being choked, drowned, or suffocated all felt alike.

I didn't remember Lucifer lifting me up from the water or rushing me to the side of the lake. What I do remember is coming too and spitting out two lungs full of water. I was gasping for air and still felt the memory of my last death creeping up on me. I was thrashing about, trying to fight off the impending death. I coughed and coughed but still couldn't get a breath. Two hands grabbed my shoulders and set me up to where I coughed and heaved more water out of my lungs. I sat there and sobbed. There was no grand life flashing before your eyes as they made it out in the movies. There's just death. I finally opened my eyes and saw it was Lucifer who held me in his arms. I looked around for Incaendiel. I was desperate to see his face. Panic shot through me, and I tried to get up to run for him. *Where was he?* Lucifer held me in his arms and wouldn't let me go.

My eyes came into focus, and I looked around me. It looked worse than it did yesterday when he set it on fire. Everything was burned to a char. There were wing imprints on the ground where every angel that had been killed had lain and died. I scanned around my surroundings and found Sam and Azazel knelt over a body. I felt my heart stop from fear.

"No!" I screamed.

I tore from Lucifer's arms and ran, stumbling over the rocks. I cut my feet fairly well, but I didn't care. I had to get to his side. I knelt beside him. He wasn't breathing, and he wasn't moving.

"No, no, no, no!"

I rocked back and forth, crying over his body. Sam and Azazel looked at me with tears in their eyes. I looked down at his chest, and right beside a scar was a puncture wound the same size and shape. Dean. He had stabbed him again and got away. He had to have pierced his heart. I threw myself on top of his body, sobbing. I covered the wound with my hand, trying to stop the blood from pouring from it. I began

159

to do chest compressions, but all it caused was more blood to pour from the wound. *Why didn't they just let me die? It was over. There's nothing we can do anymore.*

My chest started to hurt. Not an emotional hurt but an actual searing pain. It grew in intensity, and it felt like my heart was being ripped from my chest cavity.

"AHHHH!" I screamed, grabbing my chest.

Lucifer ran to my side as I doubled over, barely catching a breath.

"What's wrong with her?!" Lucifer screamed as I thudded to the ground.

He knelt beside me as I convulsed in sheer agony. It felt like my body was on fire!

"Her light is dying. There's nothing we can do," Sam said, holding my thrashing body.

Azazel sucked in her breath and squeezed her eyes shut as the tears came pouring out.

"There has to be something!" Lucifer rumbled.

He grabbed my hand, but my convulsions ripped me from his grip. He picked my body up and held me to his chest.

"AHHHHH! IT BURNS!!!!!" I screamed. The pain was so unbearable.

I felt the life leaving my body. Death had always been a touchy subject with me, especially since Gramms had died. *Who would have thought at eighteen*

I would be dealing with my own?

"INCAENDIEL!!!!!!" I called out with every ounce of energy I had.

The light was fading out as the pain grew more and more intense. In barely a whisper, I said out loud, "I love you." *My firefly.*

CHAPTER 12

*L*ove can be Stronger than Death itself

"YOU DIED for me to live today, but you didn't know that I would die with you. I cried out your name in pain, and with my final breath confessed my love for you. Our bodies touched one last time, I breathed out life and you heard my cry. You returned to me but the time was nigh, now my heart will never be thine."

I DIDN'T KNOW if it was her call out to my soul rising to the burial in the sky or if Mother found a way to heal me, but as soon as I heard her scream out my name, her parting words to me, I was sucked back into my body. I sat up and looked down at my chest as the wound began to heal on its own. That was really weird; in human form, we didn't have this power. Sam and Azazel stared at me wide-eyed.

"You're supposed to be dead! We saw you die! It's impossible!" Azazel exclaimed in shock and doubt while tears still streamed from her eyes.

I looked over to my side and saw Sophie lying in Lucifer's arms. She wasn't moving, and from what I could tell, she wasn't breathing.

"What happened?!" I demanded.

I tore her from his grasp. I wrapped my arms around her as I pulled her into me.

"When you died, her grace died. She screamed and convulsed. She yelled out your name right before she took her last breath." It was Lucifer who answered.

I ran my hand over her face. This couldn't be happening. There were too many times I had held her lifeless body in my hands. This time, there was no coming back. She was gone forever. I bent over the top of her crying. I howled out to Father.

"How could you! How could you kill one of your children!"

I felt the dark circling me, suffocating me. I didn't

care if it overtook me now. *What was the point of fighting any longer?* Father won. We would never receive our light back now. I didn't care. I had sacrificed so much for my brothers and sisters in the hope that they would return to the light, with or without me.

My tears fell like a rushing river. Foliage sprang up all around me where the fire had leveled it. Storms tore through the lake as rain, hail, and whirlwinds popped up. I felt a hand on my shoulder, one I knew all too well.

"Incaendiel, my son, do not let it overtake you. It is not hopeless yet." Mother always showed up during one of my fits.

"How can you say that? Her grace is gone! She can't return!" I stared down at her as my tears fell and dripped on her face. "She's...she's dead!" I heaved out. "This is all my fault. If I hadn't left the summit, she would be fine. Everything I have been through, we did for everyone else. She wouldn't have had to have gone through everything that bastard of a father has put her through. All this was for a plan we thought we would succeed with in the end. It's bullshit!"

I stared up at the darkening sky filled with lightning. It was a cue that he heard what I had to say.

"All you have to say for yourself is a damn

thunderstorm!"

Mother backed away from me as I started to talk to Father.

"You think that you are so perfect and everyone should bow down to your feet. Your lost children pine after your love, and all you do is rewrite us as demons into the minds of humans! The only evil person in existence is you! You locked her away in a tower and made her suffer unbearable deaths I wouldn't wish on anyone. You're the true monster of evil!"

Lightning crackled down in response.

"You do not scare me anymore! Your lightning bolts mean nothing to me!"

The lightning storm receded, and as my emotions came under control, the sky returned to blue. Everyone stared at me, baffled by my outburst at our father.

I looked down at her face and brushed the hair away, tucking it behind her ear. It was a simple gesture I have always done, but now it was the last thing I could do for her. I put my forehead to hers and cried more.

"I'm sorry, my love. I lost you, my other half, the only thing that made me whole. I'm sorry. I should have listened to you. I couldn't bear the thought of you being taken by them. I didn't expect what happened to unfold."

I rocked her body in my arms.

"I would take it all back if I could. Everything! I will not let you die in vain!"

I lay her body down, leaned down, and kissed her lips once more. My soul beckoned to her. I sat there on bent knees and placed my head in my hands. My mind reached out to the empty space and pleaded with everything I held inside as power.

"Please, don't leave me! Please, come back to me!"

A blinding flash lit the entire valley, and everyone had to shield their eyes. Most would have thought Father was making a grand entrance; however, the light didn't come from the sky. It came from my heart. Every time I watched her die, every time I had to endure her leaving me, it came out like an explosion. The raw energy of the light was sending nearly everyone toppling over. Azazel grabbed onto Sam and shut her eyes from the blinding light. A tidal wave of energy went off in the valley. The ground trembled, and the mountain near the lake began to topple from the blow. With a final burst, it disappeared. I fell to my side in exhaustion. Everything went black once more.

When I awoke, I was back in the Glade. I had a horrible headache, but it didn't feel anywhere near the amount of heartache that throbbed within my shattered heart. I shut my eyes and lay my arm back over the top of them to keep the light out. I didn't want to live. I just wanted to lie here and die so I could be with her.

"I saw you wake up. You can't fool me." The voice sang throughout my mind causing me to bolt upright in my bed.

My eyes searched the room for the owner of the voice. My eyes stopped when they rested on hers. She stood up and walked over to my bed. This had to be a dream, or I was hallucinating.

"No, you're not hallucinating. I'm real, and I'm alive." She smiled down at me, stroking my hair.

What now? She can read my thoughts without me telling her?

"Yup."

Wow, there went privacy.

She giggled. She leaned in closer and planted her lips on mine. The same wonderful electricity ignited between us. She pulled away and bent down to my ear and whispered, "I love you."

It sent a frenzy through me, and I pulled her in closer, kissing her, running my hands all over her. I sat up and flipped her beneath me, pinning her to the bed and kissing her deeper. She returned every mad kiss with a more rushed one.

There was no way this was real.

"It's real, my love."

The sound of her voice in my head made my heart throb. I kissed her, trailing my lips from her mouth to her neck. She was practically tearing my clothes off when someone cleared their throat.

"Ehem, don't mind me over here in the corner." Lucifer chuckled, and I saw her face redden.

Oh, how I feared I would never see that look on her face again. I pried myself from her with every ounce of willpower I had. I groaned inwardly as I pushed my dirty thoughts of her aside.

"How long have I been out?" I asked, looking between the two of them.

"Almost a week," he replied. "You nearly depleted your grace, returning hers to her."

I touched her face and murmured, "It was worth it."

"You two go beyond any angels I have ever witnessed. Even Mother is baffled; no angel has ever healed themselves in human form. Father is furious!" Lucifer laughed.

"I bet he is," I said snidely. "What about her memories? I blinked them here before they could touch them. Were they able to get in and find them?"

Lucifer and Sophie exchanged glances. "There's only a little under half a jar of memories left for her now."

"What do you mean half a jar!? I only used one!"

I was furious. Without those memories, the hope was still not there.

"There's only half a jar because most of them returned to me when you returned my grace. I don't know how you did that, but you did." She smiled at me and then punched me in the arm. "You could have told me I met Lucifer while he was Jesus! No wonder he gave me those crazy looks when I was referencing the Bible. He thought they were my memories."

"I couldn't tell you what you didn't know from your own memories." I pretended her punch hurt and rubbed my arm, smiling wickedly at her. "So, now what? I'm sure Father wants my head on a platter for the damage I did back at the lake."

Lucifer's face grew serious. "There have been rumors that he requested you to be punished for your actions. Mother has been thinking it over." His face looked grim.

"Oh, I should be punished for defending myself against a fleet of brothers that he sent to kill me, but his army doesn't answer for the maiming and killing of humans." I puffed and shook my head.

"You know Mother is more honorable than Father, but she does know your actions were warranted from self-defense. Not to mention, as you said, they were sent to kill you and had succeeded." He looked at Sophie. "The bond you two share is the most powerful bond I have ever seen. She called out your name, begging you back. You were dead! I watched as you returned to her. It was remarkable!"

Samael walked into the room and looked at me solemnly. "Mother wishes to see you since you have awakened. Sophie, you are to stay here." He looked over to Lucifer. "You too."

I stood and walked over to Samael. I turned around, smiled at Sophie, and then proceeded through the door. Samael walked in utter silence. I wasn't sure if that was a good thing or a bad thing. We entered the throne room where Mother went during the day to watch the world. She sat in her chair made from a large lily and lily pad.

"My son, I see you have finally awakened. You slept so long; we were fearful you wouldn't wake back up."

She stood from her chair and walked over to me. She wrapped her arms around me, and I could feel her love radiate through me. Again, I didn't know if this was a good thing or a bad thing.

"You may leave, Samael. We have much to discuss." He nodded and left the room.

"Did the others explain the reasoning behind my actions at the lake?"

She nodded, but her face still did not show the warmth I expected.

"I will accept whatever punishment you deem fit for my actions then."

She stared into my eyes. Her eyes were always so hard to read, and I was certain mine were to her as well.

"You have received punishment enough for your actions. I do believe being killed was punishment enough."

She opened the door behind the throne and walked out into the open field that lay beneath the mountain. The Glade was named for its lustrous gardens and fields that sprang up beneath the mountain base. None of the fallen ones knew if the cave spiraled down and then up or if the fields and meadows really did exist below the Earth. I followed her through the meadows as she walked. I had no clue what she meant by telling Samael that she had much to discuss with me if she hadn't intended to punish me for my actions.

We came to a clearing in the meadow where there was an enormous weeping willow growing. It looked as if it held up the sky here. She sat under the willow tree and motioned for me to do the same. I walked over, sat down beside her, and looked around our surroundings. Never had I been to this portion of the Glade; Mother normally didn't let anyone through the door. I wondered why she let me come with her this time...

As I watched the meadow, it began to change from the summery scene it was suspended in into an autumn one. The leaves on the trees began to turn from green to yellow to a beautiful shade of reddish-orange. Each one that fell was caught by the breeze and carried to the center of the meadow. Once every flower had disappeared from the meadow, it began to grow insanely cold. The wind began blowing and howling with snow falling everywhere around. It blanketed the meadow, covering the pile of leaves and fields in thick blankets of powdered ice. Everywhere in the meadow, the seasons changed from one to the next, except for under the willow tree we sat.

"Oftentimes, I come out here and watch the seasons change before my eyes. It's so much more beautiful seeing them change, as if the world was spinning through them that fast. It reminds me of how time is different in the summit as opposed to here on Earth. I have kept this part of the meadow to myself, for it reminds me of who I really am as opposed to who I have become."

I watched her as she spoke. She never talked to us children about herself and the darkness, not since the fall she hasn't.

"There were times I would come out here and cry a river that would wrap around the entire Glade. It has been many years since I have felt the urge to cry over leaving the summit behind."

Her eyes began to mist over.

"There were more important things to cry about than leaving the summit this past week."

As her tears fell, they found their way to the river that was rolling along the edge of the meadow.

"We all feared we had lost you, Incaendiel. I felt Sophie's cries for you. I appeared moments before your soul returned back to your body. I watched her last few moments, her dying breath call out to you, and tell you she loved you. I saw your soul fight against the claws of death to return to her. I have never seen an angel capable of doing that. You are the first one to die a mortal death and then actually return back. Even Lucifer left his mortal body before they plunged that spear into him."

I didn't know if her eyes looked at me in admiration or fear, but she stared at me. She stared long and hard.

"I thought the darkness had completely engulfed you when you found her dead. I saw it swirl your body and grow thicker, darker, and impenetrable. Your grace burst through that darkness and nearly exploded the valley. There has never been an angel with your power. You restored her grace and part of her light. Those are powers neither Alpha nor I have."

She fell silent.

"What does that mean for me?" I asked timidly.

I didn't know if I wanted to know the answer. She didn't answer me immediately. I could see that she was pondering on it herself. When she looked at me, a tear fell from her eyes.

"I believe it means that you are truly his adversary, not I."

The words stung.

"There is no way I love the father more than you

do, Mother."

She bowed her head.

"You called out to him in a fit of rage. He heard your plea to him. No angel has the power to call out to him the way you did." She paused. "In order to understand the light, you have to first understand the darkness. You have been battling the dark for many, many years. I have watched you overcome it numerous times. Never once did I know that the darkness was already within your heart. The dark cloud we have always believed to have been engulfing you, sucking you in, was truly you emanating the darkness that was already within you."

"If that is so, then how am I to return to the light? No one that holds darkness in their heart can be a child of the light." I felt the world crashing down around me.

"You are different. You use the dark to seek the light, which is an old and wise power. The universe at one point in time was nothing but darkness before your father had light spring forth throughout it."

She turned to me and peered deeply into my eyes, into my soul. I could feel her eyes piercing my insides.

"You are the darkness, and Sophie is the light. Together, you two are a force the world has never before seen. Apart, the two of you cannot survive without one another. You two are the true yin and yang energies that have kept the universe from falling in on itself."

"What about the fear of the darkness consuming me? I heard you all speak of it."

I was confused by all she was telling me.

"Our fear has always been that at the last moment, the darkness would overtake your light. I thought it meant your actual angelic light."

She stood up and looked out across the valley.

"Well, what light could it possibly mean?"

I had no idea what her riddles spoke.

"We have to keep the darkness from engulfing Sophie."

This was something I already knew.

"Of course, we have to keep her from the darkness. She isn't a fallen one. But what does that have to do with anything?"

I was becoming slightly irritated with the banter between us. She smiled at me.

"I know my riddles have always worked your nerve. But listen closely. An angel of the light can never be engulfed by the dark. They turn evil. They turn into the creatures that your father convinced the world that we are."

"What does that have to do with my light?"

She smiled once more.

"Sophie is your light."

I stood there frozen. *What?*

"Sophie is your light in the dark. She is the one saving you from the dark. Without her light, we are all doomed. We will, one by one, turn into those hideous creatures. She is the beacon of hope for not just returning to the summit but for survival."

I stood there thinking to myself. *If the dark existed within me, how could I keep her from the dark?*

I knew what I had to do without even trying for an answer. I didn't like the idea, and it tore me in two to make the final decision.

"Make sure Lucifer gets the rest of her memories into her."

I started to walk from the meadow.

"Where are you going, my son?"

She was confused, and I could hear it in her voice.

"You said I had to keep her from the dark, right?"

She nodded her head with her brows furrowed.

"I'm the dark."

Her eyes widened in the realization of what my plans were.

"But we need both of you to get the portal open!" She called out to me.

I took a deep breath. "We will open the portal, but I cannot be around her in the meantime. Not while she is receiving more of her angelic memories. The more memories she receives, the less human she becomes."

"What if she needs you? What if we need you?"

I had never seen Mother so torn before.

"I'm just a call away. She knows how to reach me."

I walked through the entrance we had taken into the meadow and back into her throne room. I made my way through the corridors and snaked my way up the staircase. When I was far away enough to where she couldn't run for me to make me change my mind, I called to her.

"Sophie?"

I waited for her reply.

"Where are you?"

I sucked in a deep breath as I walked.

"I have to keep my promise to you."

"What promise is that?"

I didn't know how I was going to force the next few words into a sentence.

"I have to go away for a while. Lucifer will be with you to protect you."

"Why?! You can't leave me behind, Incaendiel. You can't leave me!"

Her pleas were tearing my heart in two.

"I have to. It's the only way to keep you safe."

A tear slid down my face.

"I'm safe with you! Please, Incaendiel, nothing good ever comes from us being apart. You promised me you would never leave me!"

"You're not safe with me right now! You're getting closer to your angelic form and becoming less human. I must stay away. Until you are fully prepared to open the portal with me, I cannot be around you. I'm sorry!"

Tears rolled from my eyes. This was the hardest thing I think I could ever do, leaving her. It was something I had always promised her I would never do; the reason I was at her side each time she died a human death.

"Sophie, I love you...I just can't be with you."

No response was even harder than her pleas. I understood, though. I understood that she was hurting. She needed to understand this was the best thing for her.

CHAPTER 13

If you Love Them Set Them Free

"WHERE HAVE you gone my love, when you whispered to me forever? When will I see you my love, when you said you would leave me never? You have gone away from me, tearing me down to a brittle house of cards. My heart lays in pieces.... what am I to do now, my love?"

HE'S GONE. He's gone! He left me here. I can't believe that he thinks he is a danger to me. Why would he think that? He saved me! He returned my grace and light! I died, and he brought me back from the abyss. I ran through the corridors and up the spiral staircase. I saw him as he told me he loved me, and then he was gone. I threw myself on the ground in tears. My heart was breaking. *He can't leave me. I need him. I need him now more than ever.*

All the years of memories came flooding to my mind, bringing me to my knees. It was always him begging me to stay. It was him telling me how much he needed me, how much he wanted me, how he would never leave without me. I always turned away from his love. *Is that what he is doing now? Is he turning away from my love?* I needed answers and had no idea who to ask. I lay my head down on the grass, brought my knees to my chest, and cried. I cried like I had never cried before. I felt abandoned. I felt utterly alone. I felt like I had been flying on cloud nine, and the cloud was ripped from my feet. I plummeted deep into my pain.

He can't leave me. He promised me! A hard-learned lesson of "promises were meant to be broken" was not what I wanted to fill my head. I don't know which hurt worse, the pain from my light dying or the pain from my heartbreaking. If you could die from a broken heart, this would be the moment of my final death. I knew, in reality, I wouldn't die, but so many famous people had died from heartache and heartbreak. Deep down, I felt like he didn't want me. Out of all the years of him staying away from me, it was easy to convince myself this was the reason he left. He didn't want me. It was the only feasible answer.

I felt myself gathered up into arms. It wasn't the arms I wanted. It wasn't his arms. I was carried down the spiral staircase and into the room I had run from to stop Incaendiel. I was laid down on the bed. I didn't speak. I didn't move. I was numb to everything. Every voice I heard didn't have emotion in it. Every sound didn't have the same luster to it. The world to me was becoming as dead as the feelings I held within me.

"We have to take her home before she kills us all with gloom!" Sam yelled.

Even his yelling voice didn't have the same effect that it had before.

"There is no way we can take her back home in this condition. Every human in the town will weep for no reason and continue to do so until she stops crying!"

Lucifer's anger wasn't as angry as expected.

"Well, what do you propose we do? Drag him back here? He cloaked himself! Not even Mother knows where he is!"

He wanted to hide from everyone. He wanted to make sure no one would drag him back to me. My heart sank lower in my chest. I heard Lucifer groan.

"Quit speaking like that in front of her, or she will kill us all from despair!"

How can my emotions affect them the way they are? There's nothing special about me. I wasn't like Incaendiel. Just thinking about his name makes my heart ache more. I felt my body sinking into the bed as if it were mud. I wanted to be completely numb. I didn't want to feel this pain. It wasn't real. It had to be a dream. Incaendiel wouldn't leave me behind. He had never left me behind in all our years fighting this battle. The tears began to roll from my eyes again. It was like it was on a timed sprinkler system. I couldn't control them.

"The only person ever able to take away her pain is the one that left!" Sam shouted at Lucifer.

They both looked down at me, but I ignored their stares. Lucifer sat down beside me and stroked my hair. Sam scowled and walked out of the room. Everything grew quiet around me. I saw Lucifer's lips moving, but no sounds escaped them. The silence was engulfing me, suffocating me. I couldn't bear it any longer. I sat up from the bed and bolted out the door. I topped the staircase in seconds, it seemed, and dashed from the cave.

I ran. I ran the way I did the night Gramms died. Mom was so angry and hurt when the police brought me home. I didn't care, though; I had to run, just like I do now. I ran, expecting to tire out, but I didn't. It was as if I had some new energy that I had never before possessed. I didn't know where I was running to. My course changed every so often when I thought I was close to stopping. My feet had a mind of their own. I wasn't breathless; I wasn't tired. I felt free for the first time in a long time. Each step I took seemed to gain a few extra feet. The terrain whipped by me in nearly a blur. I closed my eyes and trusted my feet to take me where I needed to go. The air on my face blew so fast it was exhilarating. When I finally opened my eyes, I was no longer running on the ground. I was flying.

I felt like I was millions of miles up in the air. I pushed forward, and my wings flew with such speed that it took my breath away. I loved it. I soared and tumbled through the air. When my tears fell from my face, they fell as rain across the land. Even in the excitement of my newfound wings, the despair that ran through me still coursed through my veins. *Where could he have gone?* I flew for miles and landed at the lake. Once again, he had used his powers to grow the foliage back around it. I looked around the entire mountain for him, but he was not there.

I flew back to the edge of the lake and sat down. I was stupid to have a sliver of hope that he would be here. He wouldn't have gone anywhere we would have thought to look for him. The tears started again, wisping their way from my eyes down my face. Each one dropped into the lake, making tiny waves and rippling out across the lake. I closed my eyes and breathed in deeply. *When would he come back for me?* I missed him terribly. I felt like my entire life was ripped from my hands. I knew this was what heartbreak felt like. It had to be. My heart throbbed the same way when Gramms died. The sad part was that he didn't die; he just left.

He was my protector, and he left me vulnerable. I wasn't sure which hurt worse, the fact that he left me when I needed his protection the most or that he left me when the love between us had begun to intensify. Go figure, the moment I gave myself completely to someone, gave them my heart, they just walked out of my life. I understood there was more to the entire situation than just an eighteen-year-old's first romance, but that's exactly what this is. My soul may be millions of years old, but right now, it was trapped in a body that wasn't even a measurement on a ruler compared to it. I may remember a good portion of my past lives, but they didn't compare to my experiences in this one.

How long will I have to wait for his return? Will he ever return? Will he just let me die on my nineteenth birthday and say screw it all?

"How could you even think that one!?"

I sucked in a breath as the tears wanted to fall. Just the sound of his voice in my head made me want to ball up and die.

"Sophie, I love you, do not doubt that. I just can't be around you; I can't be with you right now. I'm dangerous to you."

I wanted to answer him, but even the voice in my head quivered with sadness. I closed my eyes as another tear slid down my cheek.

"You can't be with me, or you don't want to be with me?"

Silence filled my head. My heart yearned to hear his response, to hear his voice in my head.

"Please, come back to me."

I wished the fantasy I had played out in my head would have happened; a hand would brush my cheek, and I would open my eyes to see him. When I opened my eyes, there was no one there; there was no comforting hand upon my cheek. I was utterly alone. His voice was gone from my head. How I longed for it to speak to me again, but I knew he wouldn't unless I really needed him. Somehow, I knew he felt my heartache and pain. *How could he deal with what I felt? Is this what he felt all those years when I let the other angels get close to me?*

I sat by the edge of the lake for hours. I didn't want to leave. This was our place. This was where all the moments that meant something between us had

185

sparked. I could feel him here, and that's all I wanted. The day turned quickly into night, but I didn't budge. I didn't sleep. I just sat there and numbly stared out at the lake. The night felt like an eternity in the darkness. I sat there and thought of our last day at the lake, the moment when I was going to tell him out loud how I felt. I was so nervous, so scared of saying it out loud. Of course, I knew how he felt for me. We are bound by eternity with each other. But the hesitance of that moment, of the utterance of those words, was because of this very moment. I was afraid of being alone. Now, look at me.

I watched the stars reflected in the lake water. I hoped to see him hovering above the trees in the background. I turned quickly, thinking I might catch a glimpse of him somewhere. There was no such luck. He never came to kiss me goodbye or tell me in person that he was leaving, yet he wanted to hear the words I love you out loud. This slightly angered me, and I enjoyed the anger. I guess I was going in the order of the chart for grief. I didn't care.

I sat there all night. The sun began to peek out behind the mountain, signaling dawn. I didn't move. I felt someone walk up behind me, but I didn't care who it was. It could have been Dean for all I cared because I didn't care. The person sat down beside me. It wasn't him which sent my heart further into pieces.

"Did you sit out here all night?"

Of course, it was Lucifer. It seemed like he stalked me everywhere I went. If I didn't know any better, I'd swear we had a thing going on in the summit. I didn't answer his question. I sat there quietly.

"Sophie, you have to snap out of this. You're going to grieve your grace away!"

I didn't respond to him. As a matter of fact, it had been an entire day since I had said a single word out loud to anybody. I felt his hand on my shoulder, and it angered me.

"Sophie?"

"Leave me alone!" I shouted and pushed his hand from me.

My voice echoed powerfully through the mountain. I figured he would have flitted away, but he stayed put.

"Why don't you people ever listen? I didn't want to be a part of this in the beginning. I was dragged into it. I couldn't even live a normal life growing up because of this whole mess! The only people who have ever shown interest in me was a conniving, bastard angel and Incaendiel. Where are they now? Nowhere to be seen. I couldn't even have a normal experience as a human while on Earth. Everything has always circled around this damn year! I'm tired of it. I'm tired of being told what needs to be done and how it should be done. I'm tired of feeling like I was abandoned. I'm tired of always grasping but never fully receiving him into my arms. We can finally be together after my eighteenth birthday, and he runs away! He leaves me!"

The tears poured from my eyes. It was centuries of pent-up anger, frustration, envy, and disappointment. My heart did more than just ache; it hurt.

We sat there for a while in silence until he was able to pry me away. He carried me home and put me in my bed. Somehow, they had cast a glamour to make my mom think I had been in bed sick with the flu or something the entire time. School was starting the next day, and everything had to seem like nothing in my life had changed. I stayed in bed even though mom pestered me to get up. I had no energy. I felt like the life had drained from me. The day turned quickly into night, and I didn't feel like starting school at all the next day. Mom agreed it would be best for me to stay home as well.

Night turned into morning, and the days just seemed to flutter by. I never once moved out of my bed. I had missed the first week of school, but I didn't care. I didn't need school. Soon, Mom began to think I had mono and requested for an in-home tutor until I felt well enough to go back. I would lay in bed and stare out the window while the teacher would drone on and on over the studies. The weeks turned into months, and I spent each day in a fog.

"Sophie, I don't know what's wrong with you, but you need to snap out of your funk. Get out of bed, shower because the good Lord knows you need one, and come down for breakfast. It's not a request." I pried myself from the bed and trudged to the shower. The hot water didn't even soothe my broken soul.

When I appeared downstairs, Mom had me a plate of food and a cup of coffee sitting on the table. I grimaced and sat down. I picked up my fork and rolled the food around the plate.

"So, are you going to tell me what's really going on?" she asked, peering over her cup of coffee at me. I was silent. I didn't want to talk about anything. "Sophie, he's just a boy. These things happen."

"You wouldn't understand."

My eyes never left my plate.

"You went on a date with Isaiah, and since then, I haven't seen him around. I understand. I thought you two were going to hit it off as well. That boy was always wrapped around your finger when you were kids."

She sat her cup down and touched my hand lying on the table.

"Your first heartbreak is always the hardest. I know he was your first boyfriend, but you have to get through this, sweetie."

It took every ounce of willpower I had in me not to break down and cry. She wouldn't understand the true reasons behind everything. She didn't believe in the family Bible and would have me committed if I told her the truth. I mumbled that I was fine and excused myself from the table. She watched me stand from the table with worry written all over her face. I had to get outside. I needed air. I stepped outside and closed my eyes, breathing in deeply.

"You should have expected the pep talk. It would have been easier."

Lucifer sat reading a copy of Socrates' Philosophy on the porch. I walked over and sat down beside him.

"I didn't think she would have remembered it." I sat there, brooding. "So, what happens now? How do I do the school thing when I've missed so many days?"

He closed the book he was reading and chuckled. "The school thing will be easy. There will be five of us there to protect you. Since Sam and Azazel are first and second in command and, of course, well known at the school, they kept to the same roles they had. Metatron, Michael, and I filled in as transfer students. There will be around the clock protection from at least one of us, so Azazel persuaded the Secretary at the school to insure it. There's still time for you to return and continue on as a normal student."

"What about Dean and the other angels?"

He stiffened when I mentioned their existence. It was as if he had forgotten until now.

"Dean is already causing mischief at the school along with four others as well. As long as you stay away from them and don't get sucked into their lies, you will be fine."

He smiled at me.

"Why are you so nice to me, Prince of Darkness?" I laughed, and he playfully socked me in the arm.

It was the first time in forever I had a smile form on my face.

"Someone has to be. Who better than the compassionate, all-loving son," he murmured as he looked me in the eyes.

He brushed the hair from my face.

"The one that protected you while you were locked away in the tower."

His thumb brushed alongside my jawline, and my heart skipped a beat. I spiraled into a dark hole.

"Incaendiel will return for me. I know he will."

My voice was more reassuring than what my heart and mind were. Lucifer stood before me. His eyes danced in mine.

"He will never return," he said.

"Why do you keep saying that?! He will return! He must return! Or, as you said, I will die!" I began to tear up.

"You misunderstood my words, my darling. I didn't say if he didn't return, you would die. I said if he did return...you would die."

My eyes searched his face for a lie. No one could lie in his presence, so did that mean he was incapable as well?

"You do not speak the truth!" I yelled.

He reached out with his hands and pulled me into his chest.

"You know it is true, Sophie. You just must believe it. His darkness will consume you. It will consume us all!"

It felt nice to be in someone's arms. It felt even nicer that they belonged to Lucifer.

"What if I wanted to die for him to regain his light?" I asked.

"No! I won't let you!" He shook me when he said it.

"His darkness is my fault. I promised him his return. I promised we would reunite. I promised."

I broke down crying.

"Not all promises can be kept, my darling," Lucifer said as he swept me up in his arms.

He wiped away my tears and then kissed me.

I snapped back from the black hole with a pounding headache. "Did you slip a damn memory in?"

192

His eyes widened in surprise. "No, I didn't. What did you remember?"

I thought back to the memory and looked at him. *Did I really betray Incaendiel with Lucifer? I couldn't have!* The waves that had been rolling in on me when Incaendiel left crashed on top of me. I felt like throwing up.

"What did you do?! Take advantage of me alone in the tower?! Try to get the details from me where the Garden is?! You snake!"

He looked at me bewildered, and then it sank in what memory I had.

"You...saw us...didn't you?"

He looked down at the ground when he asked, his cheeks flushed. I smacked him across the face.

"How could you use me like that?"

I was sad, angry, and confused all in one.

"I didn't use you. We spent 2,000 years together in that tower together. What did you expect to happen?"

I couldn't look him in the face I was so guilty.

"You were guilty then, too, just so you know. You always told me once Incaendiel returned, you would be with him, not with me."

He touched my hand.

"It can still be like that. Until he returns..."

I jerked my hand away. I didn't know what I wanted or what I wanted to do. There was a piece of myself that was drawn to Lucifer. Not a strong magnetic pull like with Incaendiel, but a connection.

"You just want to pick up where we left off? Like there hasn't been any type of change? Incaendiel will return. He will return to me here on Earth, and he will make it back to the summit with all of us. I'm not yours, Lucifer. I was not created alongside you. I'm not Sophia!"

I was sure of his return. Lucifer dropped his head. I knew that last line would hurt him most of all, but I didn't care.

"When you recover more memories, let me know. We will talk then. Otherwise, just don't speak to me anymore."

He blinked away. He was hurt. I had hurt him. I hurt him the way Incaendiel had hurt me. *Did he know? Did he know about my betrayal?* Just thinking the word sent a wave of nausea and despair through me. I had to go somewhere, anywhere. I couldn't let anyone see me in the mess I was in. I hadn't slept in months; I was an emotional wreck, and I needed space from this whole situation.

I walked to my car and hopped in when the passenger door swung open. Michael climbed into the seat beside me.

"We have much to talk about, Sophie."

He looked over at me, and his look wasn't friendly in the least. I looked down at his lap, and he was holding my jar of memories.

"What are you doing with that?"

I didn't understand why he had the jar. Apparently, I no longer needed to be spoon-fed the memories; they just leapt into my mind.

"Drive to the lake."

It wasn't a request but rather a demand.

"What's at the lake?" I asked.

I wished I hadn't pissed Lucifer off. I sent a mental cry to him, inquiring about the lake. I didn't know if it was just a thing between Incaendiel and me or not.

"Just drive."

He stared out of my windshield. I had an eerie feeling with him. I didn't feel safe. Nonetheless, I put the car in reverse and backed out of the driveway. I steered the car in the direction of the mountain. The car was silent. I took quick glances over at Michael as he sat there staring out the window.

"Why do you have the jar of memories? I don't need it to get them back. I've been having memories return on their own."

He didn't reply.

"Why won't you talk to me?"

He turned and glared at me, and then he smiled a sly smile.

"It was so easy to fool you all. Even Metatron honestly thought I had fallen to help. He's so stupid."

195

My heart stopped. *No! He couldn't lie in front of Lucifer.*

"There are ways around Lucifer's gift."

It was as if he knew what I was thinking.

"Incaendiel timed it perfectly. The best thing he did was leave you. It returned your angelic grace. I waited until you were completely broken in half. I followed you flying through the skies the day he left. You're faster than I remembered, but I kept up pretty well."

He followed me? So, the odd sensation I was hoping to be Incaendiel was him.

"Since you're nearly a complete angel again, I can force-feed these memories to you and not worry about your brain exploding. Once you remember each and every one of them, I'm taking the Garden for myself."

No! Incaendiel, wherever you are, you need to get your ass back here. This is serious! I was half hoping he would answer back, but he did not.

"Do you think Incaendiel would come for you? He abandoned you. And Lucifer!" He laughed. "Lucifer was so stupid to fall for you."

He knew? My face must have shown surprise.

"Everyone in the summit knew. We could hear you two from the castle, for Christ's sake." Then he grinned. "Or should I say for Lucifer's sake?"

So, it was more than just kissing. We...actually... Oh, come on, Sophie, your angelic soul is older than freaking eighteen.

"Lucky for me, Lucifer, and you don't have the same connection with your mind as Incaendiel. This will go off without a hitch. I told everyone you needed privacy with your memories and requested me to help. Perfect plan. No interruptions and Lucifer's too busy sulking to pay it any attention."

I realized what he had done.

"You sent me that memory of Lucifer to have me make him leave!"

He laughed in my face. I was so foolish. *What if I were to drive the car off the road? Would it buy me enough time to make it to the cave?* As if answering my question, a sharp object pointed at my side.

"Do anything stupid, this goes through you, and we do this all over again in one thousand years. Got it?"

We topped the last hill, and I turned the car into the parking lot. The lake was a good three-mile hike. Michael grabbed my hand and blinked us there. Dean and four others were there as well.

"Did you put the stakes in the ground as I said?" he asked, turning to Dean.

"They're all ready." He smiled smugly at me.

"Good. Tie her down."

I panicked.

"Tie me down? What?! Why are you tying me down?!"

Dean and one of the other angels grabbed my arms and towed me over to where I saw the four stakes driven into the ground. I struggled against their grips. Even with what strength and power that had been returned to me, I couldn't fight them off.

Where was Incaendiel? He should have shown up with me being in danger. They threw me to the ground, which knocked the breath from my lungs. I tried gulping down a breath as they tied my hands and feet to the stakes. I pulled against the ropes, but they didn't budge. I was stuck.

"They could kill me, Incaendiel! Where are you!?"

There was no answer to my call. My heart sank further into my chest.

"I thought you loved me!"

Michael walked over to me, holding the jar.

"Well, are we comfortable?"

He sat down beside me and unscrewed the lid of the jar.

"So, how shall we do this? One at a time, or all at once. I myself prefer all at once, but you are still human. All of them at once may kill you, and then we would be back at step one again."

He reached into the jar and drew out one of my memories.

He smiled a sly grin. "Oh, I do believe you would like this one indeed."

He crushed the memory in his hand and placed it on my forehead. I convulsed a little and then went down the familiar black hole.

CHAPTER 14

*W*ill Help Ever Come?

"SAVE ME! I cried out thrashing in my chains. Release me from the hold this pain has over me. Swoop in and carry me away on wings of hope. Take me to your place of safety in the heavens abode. Why must I go through this without a hero to cut me loose? I guess this time the hero isn't coming, so it's up to me to save me from doom."

I AWOKE, screaming. The group of angels that stood around me laughed. He had already given me at least ten memories back-to-back. I had truthfully lost count. I was sweating from the pain the memories were causing in my head. I turned my head heaving. I vomited up stomach acid. Even with that many memories poured into my head, the jar still looked untouched.

"Are we ready for another one?" Michael asked while he reached for the jar.

"No, no, no, please!" I cried.

I honestly didn't know if I could handle another memory. I could feel something trickling from my nose. I was getting a nosebleed. They were causing my brain to bleed. My knight in shining armor still had not shown up to save me.

"If you want to kill me, just do it already!"

He laughed at my plea.

"Killing you is not in my nature. Making you suffer is a different story."

I glared at him.

"Well, since you can't handle another memory right now, maybe you can handle some manhandling. It has been a while since we passed you around."

He bent down, brushed my hair away from my face, and tried to rub my jaw as if it were affectionate to me. I jerked my head away from his hand.

"If you touch me, Incaendiel will-"

"He will what? Is he here yet? Have you not pleaded with your mind for him to come to rescue you?"

He eyed me as I glared back.

"Ah, you have. Poor, poor Sophie. You have truly been abandoned. He's not coming for you." He sneered, and all the angels laughed.

"What did you do to him?" I glared up at him.

He matched my glare.

"Let's just say he's not making it anytime soon."

My heart sank. He had to come for me. He promised he would. Then again, I promised him a lot of things that I broke a long time ago. *Is that why he hasn't shown up? Is he making me suffer for my betrayal?*

Michael bent over me and smacked me across the face. I closed my eyes and sent my mind to a different place. He laid blow after blow against my fragile body. I squeezed my eyes shut and made myself project from the place. I must've passed out. When I awoke, Michael was sitting next to me, crushing a memory. My entire body burned and hurt.

"Back to sleep we go, my sweet."

He pressed his hand to my forehead, and down the rabbit hole, I went again.

I was at the summit. Alpha had pulled me in front of him as court was initiated.

"Sophie, you have been charged with treason. The sentence is normally stripping you of your grace and light

202

and letting you roam the earth for eternity. However, I have a far better plan for you. Since your treason was trying to help the fallen ones return, then you certainly will."

I glanced around at my brothers and sisters as I stood shackled in front of Alpha. Not a single one announced their distaste for his ruling. My eyes caught Lucifer's eyes, and he nodded his head.

I returned my look to Alpha. "I accept my punishment."

"Good, you will return to earth every one thousand years to the family of what your mother has called Guardians. On your eighteenth birthday, I will send one of my angels down to rescue you. Your brothers and sisters who have fallen will try to prevent that from happening."

I knew it was a lie. I had my vision that he didn't know about. I knew the real reason behind it.

"Will you influence my decisions while I am in human form? They do have free will."

The question struck him oddly. I could see it in his face.

"Of course, you will have your own free will."

He studied my face.

"When do I start my punishment?"

I was eager to find Incaendiel and return them home.

"Your punishment starts immediately and lasts until either side succeeds. It's up to your human decision how long your punishment shall extend. On your nineteenth birthday of each human life, you will die and return here. The second part of your punishment is to remain locked in *the tower in between incarnations."*

Everyone gasped. No one had ever lasted that long in the tower. They had never known anyone to be punished to that extent.

My eyes caught Lucifer's as I breathed in deep and heavy. His eyes didn't flicker. He just nodded.

"How soon is immediately?"

I was sucked back out of the darkness. The pain in my head was unbearable. I was dizzy, and the entire sky was spinning. Michael's hand was resting on my bare thigh. He was making circles with his finger. I couldn't even speak or scream out in protest against him, touching me again. I was too tired to do anything.

"Check her pupils. Make sure she isn't going comatose or anything," Michael ordered.

Dean bent over me, lifting my eyelids, and peered at my eyes. I stared back at him. I didn't know if they dilated or not. He just stared at me.

"Well, are they dilating?"

"I can't tell. I think we need to give her a break."

It was odd for him to take my side. I couldn't move my head really to see what all happened. I know that Michael jumped up and grabbed Dean by the shirt.

"I'm the one in charge here. You do as I say."

I tried to focus on all the other angels. They were standing a few feet away from me. The looks on their faces read that they didn't agree with Michael's tactics. I wondered if they... touched... I couldn't even finish the thought in my head as the tears began to brim behind my eyes. Michael and Dean were still gone out of my sight, and the others began to talk.

"If Lucifer or one of the others show up, we're dead!"

I had no clue what their names were. I was never introduced, and I can't remember any of the angels' names.

"Well, what do you propose we do? We can't let her go, or HE will kill us!" another replied.

"That is if Dean doesn't kill him first. Dean has nearly killed Incaendiel twice."

They were wrong. He succeeded the second time.

I licked my lips and tried to cry out to them. It came as a croak from where my throat was so dry.

"Please, let me go."

They just stared at me. I could tell they were on the ropes about what to do. One of them walked over and took out a knife. I flinched away from the blade, and he held up his hands as surrender.

"I'm just going to cut the ropes."

He took the knife to each stake and released my limbs from them. My body thudded to the ground. I had no sensation in my limbs. *How long had we been here?* I slowly rolled over on my stomach and tried to find something to cover my body with as a safety net. I groped at the ground until I felt a blanket draped across me. I looked up and smiled.

"Thank you, Brothers."

It came out as a whisper, but they nodded their heads. They disappeared. The jar of my memories was within my reach, and I grabbed it. I couldn't move anywhere, and I heard the voices of Michael and Dean returning.

What am I going to do? I was frantic. I had nowhere to hide and couldn't hide if I tried. I could barely move. Their voices were getting closer and closer. I closed my eyes and wished with all my might to be in the Glade. The strangest sensation surged through my body, and when I opened my eyes, I was in the Glade. I blinked. I couldn't believe it, *I blinked! But where in the Glade was I?* I looked around and saw no one. I was in some sort of closet.

I tried swallowing to alleviate my throat so I could cry out for some help. It was still bone dry.

"Help," I whispered. "Help."

It came out a bit louder as I croaked it out.

"Help! Help me! Someone!"

I was frantic, with tears coming down my face. I felt no safer than I had with Michael. I tried to move, but my body still groaned against it. *Oh no, what if Michael comes here looking for me? Did he know I blinked away? Does he think I just ran away?*

"Please, someone..." I was in tears. I couldn't even lift my arm to bang on the door in front of me.

The room began to spin again. I was going to blackout again. Lucky for me, I knew it wasn't a memory since I held them in the jar in my hands. The door squeaked open, and I heard a familiar voice.

"Sophie, is that you?" It was Sam. "Guys, I found her!"

He bent down to pick me up when he noticed there was a blanket wrapped around me. He peeled it back to reveal the blood and bruises left behind by Michael's torture.

"What happened to you, Sophie?" Azazel and Lucifer appeared at the door behind him.

Lucifer took one look at me and nearly crumpled. I had no clue what I even looked like. *Had Michael beaten me more while I was in and out of consciousness?* Lucifer pushed past Azazel and Sam and lifted me. He carried me out of the closet and laid me down gently on the bed.

"Who did this to you?!" he demanded.

I opened my mouth to tell him, but the words didn't want to come out. Azazel and Sam stood behind him, waiting for my answer.

"WHO?!" he yelled.

"It was Michael," I croaked out.

Lucifer's eyes went dark.

"Michael has been with us the entire time searching for you!" He was angry. "Who was it?!"

"No, no! I know what he told me." Tears fell from my face. "I know who I saw. It was Michael! He made me take him to the lake. Dean and four other angels were waiting there for us." I was crying and losing the balance of consciousness. "He forced memories into my head. He...he..." I cried.

I couldn't say it. The room began spinning again, and convulsions followed. I foamed from the mouth as my eyes rolled back into darkness.

As I came too, I heard hushed talk.

"Are you sure she said it was Michael?"

It was Metatron speaking.

"Yes, she said it was Michael." Lucifer looked solemn.

"What all did he do to her?" Metatron stood from his seat. "Why didn't Incaendiel come to help her? What is going on!?" He slung his chair across the room, furious.

"I don't know any more than you do." Lucifer looked over at me, and our eyes locked. "What I do know is someone is going to pay for this." He pulled his eyes away from mine and back to Metatron. "Does Michael have the power to create doubles of himself?" The room fell silent.

"I don't know," Metatron replied.

"What if the Michael that fell was a double? The real Michael hung back in time to strike."

"That would explain why there was a Michael in two places at once."

The room began to spin again. I leaned over the

bed and vomited.

"Go help her. We will talk later, Brother."

Metatron left the room while Lucifer walked over to me. Every bone in my body ached. I felt like I had been pushed down a flight of stairs.

"You took quite a beating. Do you remember any of it?"

He took a wet washcloth and wiped my face.

"All I remember is the agony from the memories he was forcing into my head while I was tied down."

He picked up a cup and leaned it toward my mouth. I had been craving a drink of water for forever, it seemed.

"What else happened?"

I didn't want to answer him. I shut down from that point.

"Sophie, tell me. What did he do to you?" His eyes gazed into mine.

My bottom lip quivered. "What you all did to me while I was locked away in that awful tower."

The tears streamed down my face. He squeezed his eyes tight.

"I apologized to you years ago for acting that way."

He wouldn't look at me.

"Well, that's what happens when the memory hits you. So, does the pain and anguish tied to it." He flinched away from my words. "Were you in on it with me from the beginning, or did you just use me to report to Father?"

He got up and started to walk out of the room.

"Did you think I would fall in love with you? Did you care for me? Or was I just another conquest?!"

He spun around, and I saw the fury in his face.

"I never meant to hurt you. I never used you to gain anything. It was your idea for me to report to him your treason. This was all your idea!"

He punched his fist against the wall.

"God dammit, Sophie, when are you going to realize that I truly do care about you? Does it take getting tortured for it to be even talked about?"

The room fell silent.

"Something has happened to Incaendiel."

Lucifer looked over at me with fear in his eyes.

"Why do you say that?"

"Because when I called for him, he didn't come."

Lucifer went to leave the room.

"No!"

He stopped in the doorway.

"Please, don't leave me alone in here."

It came out as barely a whisper. He turned from the doorway and walked over to my bed. His lips landed on mine, and there was a familiar feeling that soared through me. It wasn't the same feeling I felt with Incaendiel, but it was a feeling, nonetheless.

He pulled away from me and kissed my forehead.

"I will be back, I promise."

Every sensation inside of me rose, wanting to believe the words he spoke, but I knew they weren't true, and I was right. I waited in the room for three days, but Lucifer never returned. It was an empty promise, just like Incaendiel had promised.

My strength returned to me, and I finally urged myself out of the room. I found Azazel on the other side of the door as a guard. She looked at me in surprise as I walked out.

"You shouldn't be walking around!"

"Where's Lucifer?" I asked.

"The hunting party hasn't returned yet," she replied.

"Hunting party?" I didn't understand.

"They went to look for Incaendiel."

I swallowed. Lucifer is going to risk his life for the woman he loves to bring back the man she loves. *How did my life ever end up in a love triangle like this?*

There was a commotion coming from the spiral staircase. Azazel pushed me back into the room, and I heard it lock. I tried to listen through the door to what was being said on the other side. It was all drowned out by the competing voices. I sat for what seemed like hours, waiting for someone to come and release me from the room. I felt like I was locked away in the tower all over again.

Finally, I heard the key turn in the door.

"Lucifer?" I called out.

My heart dropped. It was Michael.

"Lucifer!"

"Do we really have to have this conversation again? He's not coming."

He walked slowly towards me like a cat would stalk its prey.

"Tell me, Sophie, how does it feel to be responsible for the deaths of both of the men you love?"

No, no. He was lying. They were not...they couldn't be. Michael's face melted away, and before me stood an angel that I could not place.

"What?" I was speechless and filled with dread.

"Confusing, I know, but I couldn't have them hunting my scent. If they caught wind of it, I would never succeed in this mission." He breathed in deeply. "Mmm, it's good to be the real me again. I hate shifting into the goody-two-shoes Archangels. Their compassion eats right through me." His grin was pure evil.

"Who...who are you?"

I narrowed my eyes at him studying. His demeanor felt so familiar, yet I couldn't place him.

"Why, Sister, it pains me to know you don't remember your dear, old brother, Beelzebub."

My eyes widened. I didn't remember the one I was supposed to remember, but I did remember the one the Bible spoke of. He was an evil demon.

"Ah, I see you remember at least some portion of the name, whether it be human memory or angel.

Now, back to business."

"Azazel!" I yelled out. "Sam!"

No one came.

"There's no one left, Sophie. You are truly and utterly alone. Now, to finish what we started."

He held the jar of my memories up. I backed away, squeezing my eyes shut.

"I can't do it anymore!"

I picked up a knife lying beside the bed and held it out at him. He laughed at me.

"Are you really threatening me with a knife?"

The tears ran down my face in slow trickles. *I love you, Incaendiel. We will be together again, just not this time, not this incarnation.* I lifted the knife above my head to plunge it straight toward my heart.

"No!" Beelzebub cried out as he saw me lifting the dagger.

I closed my eyes, bracing for the pain from the piercing blade, and thrust my dagger down. Instead, I felt a hand grab mine. I opened my eyes and nearly melted into the floor. Incaendiel stood before me. He knocked the knife from my hand and kicked it away. His face was filled with such pain that I had to stifle the cry, wanting to slip out. Lucifer rounded the corner just as I threw myself into his arms. Sam and Azazel had subdued Beelzebub with ropes. I buried myself deep into his chest. He pulled me in closer and closer. I opened my eyes and saw Lucifer's face. The look he had was heartbreaking. My heart felt like it was tearing in two. I squeezed myself tighter into Incaendiel's chest. He blinked me away.

CHAPTER 15

Mistakes of the Heart

"IS my love enough for you? Will you make me leave when you know what I've done? I never meant to hurt you...But I know what's done is done...Can I ever make it up to your heart? To let you know that you're the one I want? I have always loved you from the start...our existence could never be you without me, please forgive me my love...I love you from the bottom of my heart!"

I WAS afraid to open my eyes or to release the hold I had around his waist. I was afraid he would disappear or that I would be back at the lake. I had longed for his return for so long that I never thought it would happen. Tears had fallen and soaked the front of his shirt without me realizing I had been crying. He wrapped his arms tighter around me, and I felt so safe, so loved. His touch felt so real that I couldn't fight the fear any longer. I opened my eyes and found his eyes staring back at me.

"I'm sorry, Sophie. I'm so sorry. I tried to get to you. They had me in a barrier I couldn't break. I felt and saw everything they did to you."

His eyes grew dark, and I felt the anger that rippled through his body.

"I shouldn't have left you alone. I should have never left at all. My trust in others puts you in danger."

I flinched when he said the word trust. I felt the burn come to my cheeks. He lowered his eyes. He already knew what I wanted to tell him. This mind-to-mind thing sucked big time.

"Incaendiel...about Lucifer..."

He didn't even let me finish. He scooped me up in his arms and kissed me. No kiss in the world could compare to this one. It's like our bodies became one. My face flushed with heat as he moved his mouth to my neck. I felt so alive in his arms.

"Does he make you feel like this?" he asked through deep breaths.

"Does he make you feel like this?!"

He startled me to where I couldn't answer out loud. I shook my head no.

"Do you want him, or do you want me?"

This is the first time I wanted to say I want you...but deep down...I didn't know.

"Never mind what he said about me returning. This has to do with your feelings for me and your feelings for him. This will not work if your heart is not completely mine!"

He walked over to me and brushed his hand alongside my jaw and chin.

"The only thing I care about is getting you back to the summit. I don't care if you choose him over me in the end. The love between us has to be real for it to work."

I threw my arms around him and kissed him. I didn't wait for him to make the moves anymore. I slipped my tongue in his mouth and felt his arms tighten around my waist. I ripped his shirt from his body and ran my hands along his chest. My mouth moved down his neck to his chest. When I opened my eyes, we were suspended in the air. My toes danced across the clouds.

I pulled him closer to me, leaned in, and

whispered in his ear, "You should know by now who my heart belongs to."

I flew away with him fast on my heels. I zipped through the clouds with him laughing behind me. I took a dive for a river below and raced him down. Before we touched the water, he grabbed my hand and opened his wings. *Was he still in his human form?* He didn't look any different than before, but it was too dark to see anything. He pulled me in close to him and just held me.

"Please, don't ever leave me again," I whispered.

"If I told you I wouldn't, would you believe me?" he asked, stroking my hair.

"I felt a part of me die when you left. I knew you said you loved me, but my heart felt otherwise." I began to choke on my tears. "I expected you to show up at the lake that first day, then the second, and then I knew you would blink into my room." I swallowed the lump in my throat. "I was so scared you had left me forever, especially once Lucifer... it ran through my mind that's why you didn't come."

He pulled me deeper into his chest.

"Nothing in this world, jealousy, anger, nothing, would keep me from saving you if I hadn't been captured."

I wiped away my tears and prepared myself

mentally for the next question I was going to ask him.

"Do you think Lucifer's feelings for me are real?"

He tensed under the question.

"Why would you ask me that?"

His voice sounded more like he was hurt instead of angry.

"Maybe he was the one sent by Alpha to snake me away. He keeps telling me you will never return, that your darkness will kill me."

I felt his body shudder with anger.

"What memories do you have of him?"

His voice was husky.

"I had him go to Alpha to turn me over for treason. My punishment is this reincarnation thing and imprisonment in the tower in between." He landed us down on the ground.

"What happened while you were imprisoned?"

I didn't want to think of it. I didn't even want to say the words.

"I was tortured for information..."

I couldn't look at him from the shame.

"Who were the ones that tortured you?"

I closed my eyes.

"Please don't make me tell you."

He walked over and took me in his arms.

"They will never hurt you again."

I knew his eyes wouldn't lie to me.

"Who were they?"

"Too many to remember their faces. I remember Beelzebub and..."

I couldn't say it.

"And who?!" He demanded the name from me.

"Lucifer."

He dropped his hands from my waist and turned around. I saw him run his hands through his hair.

"But..."

"But what!" he snapped.

"When he was locked in the tower with me, he changed. He told me how he regretted doing what he did to me, but it was necessary so that they wouldn't find out about the plan. We..."

I couldn't finish the sentence.

"Say it."

There was no tone, no emotion.

"After some time, we developed a relationship. We made love."

He picked up a boulder and threw it across the river. It landed on the other side, exploding into tiny rocks.

"It never came close to what you and I shared, and after being locked away in that tower for millions of years, it was the only emotion I had received. I craved it."

"The angel who tortured you, you decided to

develop a relationship with."

He was angry.

"I thought it best to tell you myself than someone else."

I swallowed back the tears welling. I knew he felt betrayed. I had no excuse.

"What's happened between you two since I've been gone? Sneaking behind my back again?"

I didn't know what to say. I didn't want to answer.

"Tell me, Sophie. What am I up against? A kiss on the cheek, on the lips, some tongue, groping your chest, what?!"

"Why are you asking me this?!" I cried.

Hot tears fell down my face.

"You said that being locked up for millions of years without emotion from anyone was your excuse."

He moved in close to me.

"And!" I yelled.

"What do you think I did the entire time we have been separated? Do you think I've been screwing Azazel or any of the others?"

It dawned on me why my betrayal hurt so badly. He remained faithful to the end.

"I'm sorry, I really am. I never meant for any of this to happen the way it has. I ruined our lives together. I ruined us, I know. Just let me fix it, please!" I begged him.

I needed him to say it was okay. I needed him to say everything was fine. He was silent. I knew what he wanted to hear.

"It was just a kiss on the lips."

He dropped his head.

"When I had the memory of us in the tower, I smacked him afterward."

He looked up at me with a hint of a smile on his lips.

"We need to find out if his actions are truthful or if he is here to deceive us as well."

"Right now, we need to put some more memories in you," he said, lifting my memory jar out of his pocket.

I froze. I didn't want to do it.

"No," I said flatly.

"We have to, Sophie. They won't hurt nearly as bad since I'm putting them in you."

He walked over to me and tucked my hair behind my ear.

"You trust me, don't you?"

His eyes said he needed to hear the words.

"Yes, I trust you. I'm just not too thrilled since my brain nearly exploded last time."

I trudged along behind him as he pulled me into a cave.

"Is this where you have been hiding?"

"It's surrounded by nothing but quartz. No one

222

can sense us here."

"Before we get down to the memories, what happened to you?"

He sighed.

"I was flying out to the Glade. When you had sat for nearly two days at the lake, I couldn't stand to be away from you any longer. Four angels that are new to the mission down here captured me. They had a rope crafted from unicorn hair; the only thing powerful enough to contain an angel. They tied me up and threw me in the cave. I couldn't move, I couldn't blink. All I could do was lay there and yell for help. I wanted, no, I needed desperately to get to you. You were drowning in grief, and it was my fault. I needed you to know I didn't really leave you, even if you felt as if I did. I would never really leave you."

He caressed my face.

"Did Lucifer find you?"

He nodded.

"Does he have visions?"

He squinted his eyes and nodded.

"When I told him I thought something was wrong with you, his eyes widened with what I thought was fear. I think he saw you in a vision. He left right after it."

I left out the part where I begged him not to leave me alone, but I knew he could read it in my thoughts.

He reached out and cupped my cheek in his hand.

"I will never leave you alone again. I shouldn't have left the first time. I was just worried about me being dangerous to you. I didn't think it was dangerous for you without me by your side."

His eyes lingered on mine, and I thought I was going to explode. I wanted his touch so badly. He sat down then motioned for me to lie down on the blanket he had brought. I did as I was told and laid my head in his lap. My heart was thumping in my chest. He brushed my cheek with his hand to calm me. He reached for the jar, which was emptier than what I thought it would be.

"Are you ready?"

I nodded nervously, and he reached into the jar. He pulled a memory out, and I watched him crush it in his hands as Beelzebub had.

"I love you, Sophie."

He placed his hand on my forehead, and down the black hole I went.

This, by far, had to be the oldest memory I've recalled. The scenery was ancient in itself. I looked down at my hands and saw man hands. This isn't right. Why do I have man hands? I felt my chest and there were no breasts. I felt my crotch, and sure enough, there was an extra member there. I was standing in the middle of a field full of sheep and lambs. Am I a sheep farmer? Another young boy right around my age came sauntering up the field to me.

"Are you ready to choose which lamb is to be sacrificed?" he asked.

Sacrificed? Why am I sacrificing a lamb?

My voice deceived my questions, "Yes, Brother, and how about you? Have you harvested your best grains?"

He smiled and nodded.

"I hope Father will be pleased with our selections."

He threw his arm around my shoulder, and we walked down the hill to the tiny little cabin we lived in. Mother was ringing the dinner bell, and we needed to go eat before the celebration that night. The lamb I had chosen was tied to the house. We washed our hands in the bucket at the porch and proceeded through the door for dinner.

"At, at, did you boys wash your hands?" Mother asked.

She was so beautiful. She looked just as Lilith looked.

"Yes, ma'am, we did."

I was the one speaking to her.

"Alright, sit down and eat up. You have a celebration to attend to."

My brother and I sat and scarfed down all the food mother provided for us. We helped her pick up the dishes for the dishpan and headed outside. I ran for my lamb while my brother went for his grains. I couldn't even stop myself or look away as I slit the lamb's throat draining it of its blood. I then skinned it and cleaned it

225

up nicely for the offering. I looked over at the altar we had set up, and it looked spectacular. It had a gourd full of food setting there. His spread looked amazing with freshly baked bread and freshly plucked fruits and vegetables.

"He is sure to love your offering, Brother."

He smiled back at me.

"It surely won't top your offering. He always loves the blood sacrifices."

Something about the way he said it nauseated both me and the memory me. My Brother rang the altar bell, and there was a loud, thunderous clap from the sky.

"My favorite young brothers. How are we today?"

That voice sounded so familiar!

"We come before you, Jehovah, and offer up to thee these gifts. I bring gifts of the Earth, by grain, and by salt, I offer up to thee my hard work."

This can't be the story I think it is.

"And I offer up to thee the first newborn of my flock," I said as I raised the meat and bowed my head.

I laid the meat on the stone table, and lightning struck igniting it.

"My decision has been made."

And then the voice was gone. No, it can't be!

"Of course, he would choose your offering, Abel, Father always does. What a wonderful, early birthday present."

That means he's Cain. He didn't look angry after

Alpha had chosen my offering.

"It looks like a storm is coming, I will help you gather your sheep in the field."

No, no, don't go with him. My body didn't listen to me. It followed him automatically.

"You remember the creation story Mother and Father told us last year on your eighteenth birthday?"

This is not happening!

"Yes, Brother, it was a sad story for the Mother of Creation."

They herded the sheep down the hill.

"Abel?"

I turned around to look at Cain.

"Where is the Garden at?"

"I don't know what you're talking about, Cain. Your garden is right there beside the house. What Garden do you mean?"

Cain started to advance toward me.

"The Garden that was hidden from Jehovah, from our father, Alpha. The Garden only you know the location of. Where is it?"

Terror ran through me, and it was the terror of the moment.

"I don't know, Cain."

I stumbled backward and fell over a rock. The rock kicked up from the dirt as I tripped back on it. I hit my head, and it dizzied me. Cain was standing over top of me with the rock in hand.

"You have but one more chance, Brother. Where is

the Garden!?"

I shook with terror. I already knew how this ended.

My voice answered, "I will never tell you where the Garden is."

Cain dropped his head as if I had failed a test. I felt and heard the sickening crack as he beat me with the rock. Everything went black.

My soul arrived at the summit, and I stood before Alpha.

"Why would you not give Lucifer the location of the Garden?"

Lucifer, that snake! He had betrayed me.

"I did not recognize Lucifer in the face of the young boy I grew up to call Brother. I thought it was one of the fallen ones, so I held back."

Alpha eyed me suspiciously. Lucifer stood by his throne with his head bowed in shame.

"Tell me, Lucifer, how do you feel tainting that young man's hands with blood? He loved his brother Abel. Because of you, he will be forever remembered as Cain, son of Adam, who murdered his brother."

Lucifer flinched at my words and stalked off.

"Throw her in the tower. It is time for the second part of her punishment."

Alpha flicked his fingers. Metatron and Beelzebub escorted me to the tower.

"I am sorry for this punishment, Sister. Maybe Father will not hold out with it as long as we think,"

Metatron spoke, looking into my eyes.

I knew he was part of the revolution to get our mother and fallen brothers and sisters back into the summit.

"Do not feel pity for her, Metatron. She made her decision when she committed the act of treason."

Beelzebub was always an ass.

"Before you lock the door, let me have a word with her alone."

It was Lucifer stalking up. He pushed me into the room and shut the door.

"How dare you speak to me the way you did in court."

He was pissed.

"You took the assignment of killing me. You, of all people! I thought I could trust you! But you are just part of their scheme."

I was furious. He grabbed me by the jowls, pushed me into the wall, and stared into my eyes.

"Don't forget who is on your side in this," he hissed.

He let go of my jowls, and I backed up to the tower wall.

"Are you allowed to come check on me?" I asked.

"I will be by every so often to make sure they don't harm you. I can't make promises, though."

CHAPTER 16

own the Rabbit Hole

"HAVE you seen the white rabbit? The rabbit of purity and change? I fell down the rabbit hole once more and my fall chased him away. The colors twisted and changed, the swirling time I felt engulf me. How long until this feeling wears off and the white rabbit becomes the dream I chased away?"

IT ALWAYS SUCKED coming out of the rabbit hole. It felt like a drunken hangover. What was worse was the sense of paranoia that would wash over me. I had a heightened sense of fright when I came to this time that wasn't the paranoia's fault. I was alone in the cave. *Had they found us?* I peeked out the entrance of the cave, listening for signs of the angels. I didn't hear anything. I heard a flutter of wings and watched a figure descend. Their back was to me, but their wings were beautiful. The overcoat of feathers was black with the undercoat, a mixture of grey and black. They had a lustrous sparkle to them. When the person turned around, I was surprised who was standing there.

Incaendiel stood smiling at me, shirtless, in his true form. The silent question I had asked while we were barreling through the skies was answered. I knew exactly why he took on his true form as well. He had dropped his human form...so he could protect me. He motioned for me to come out of the cave. My eyes stayed glued to his body. He looked so different in his angelic form. Just as Metatron had been, he was toned and muscled in all the right places. His black hair seemed to shine in the night sky. As I got closer to him, his eyes were like a dark ocean gazing at me.

Every muscle in my body twitched and quaked under his gaze. My heart was beating faster than I had ever felt it beat without his touch. I felt like I had inhaled euphoria when he gazed at me. His touch sent waves instead of ripples through me. There was nothing more powerful than his touch to my skin. His lips touched mine, and I felt the Earth tremor beneath the exchange.

"Hello, beautiful," he murmured as he pulled back.

So, this was what it was like to kiss him in his true form. I could only imagine how it would feel when I was in my true form as well.

"Soon, your mortal body will melt away. You have been changing in leaps and bounds with your memories."

He stroked my hair with his hand.

"Even your hair has begun to change to the fiery, red hue it once was."

I glanced down at my hair. It had once been a dull mix between red and brown. The shine it had to it looked like magic.

I couldn't speak in his presence. It was so captivating and thrilling. I felt like I was looking at him for the first time.

"Is this what it was like when we were together before the fall?" I murmured, dazed, as he picked me up in his arms.

I felt his breath on my neck and felt like I could just pass out.

"Yes," he whispered.

It was a simple reply, but it flowed through me like warm water. He could sense that every word he spoke teased my humanity; it was written all over his face.

"This is just all too fun," he murmured through a grin.

He sat down and pulled me into his lap. He wrapped his arms around me, and it was the warmest feeling I've ever felt. I felt so loved, so protected. His eyes seemed so much brighter, staring down at me. No more worry or stress existed in them.

"So, what memory did you have this time?"

The words came out as if they were hymns of a lullaby. *I won't be able to focus around him like this.* I struggled to form my words.

"Did you know I was Abel?"

His eyes widened in surprise.

"We didn't even know Alpha sent you so soon, especially not as a boy," He contemplated on it. "This makes perfect sense. Who was it that was Cain?"

"Lucifer was given the task, as we had preplanned. Alpha was angry that I wouldn't give up the Garden to him. I told him I thought it was you all trying to pry it from me. I had to find a way to buy some time." I paused. "I believe that's when he started removing my memories."

His eyes went dark. I could tell he was thinking things over.

"Lucifer is one of us. He is not against us."

"It still doesn't mean I have to like him. He tried to betray one of his own Brothers by taking the very thing that keeps him alive."

His arms tightened around me. I loved the feel of it.

"I love you, Incaendiel. I don't tell you this enough. I can see why your faith in my love wavers, especially since I have betrayed you before."

He wouldn't look at me as I made my statement. I pulled his face to mine.

"I love you, my firefly."

His eyes sparkled, and he leaned in for a kiss.

We were interrupted by a voice. "I wondered if I would find you two here."

It was Lucifer. Not so great timing on his part. I could feel Incaendiel stiffen beneath me.

"Mother wanted to know how close you were to finishing the memories."

"Not sure, Cain. They don't come as easy as everyone thought they would."

I know my sarcasm bit into him.

"You knew what the agreement was when you stepped up to the plate."

He glared at me. I can't blame him. I had both of them wrapped around my finger at one point in time. Now, I felt like I had toyed with both of their hearts.

"Watch your tone, Brother. Do not forget whose side you fight on."

Incaendiel didn't hide the venom as it fell from his tongue.

"I bet she hasn't even told you everything from her memories."

His eyes were dark, but I could see the pain behind them.

"She told me everything. Why would you think she would hide it from me?"

Lucifer's eyes widened in surprise. I bet I would receive a memory about this one. I probably told him I would never speak of the affair.

"So, you agree that her safest bet would be to be with me?"

Fire erupted around Incaendiel.

"Ah, so it's still a touchy subject with you," he sneered.

"Enough, you two." I couldn't believe how they were acting. I looked at Lucifer, "Especially you."

"You can't tell me the kiss we shared meant nothing to you."

Oh boy. I put my hand up before Incaendiel even moved.

"Of course, it meant something to me. Yes, it tugged at a part that was buried in me."

I couldn't look over at Incaendiel's face. I could only imagine the look that sprawled across it.

"But that doesn't mean things haven't changed

since I was reunited with Incaendiel. You knew what would happen when the time came."

"How about we make the decision easier for you."

Lucifer grinned wickedly at Incaendiel.

"We don't have to fight to prove our love to her. We don't have to fight to knock one another out of the ring. When the time comes, she will choose on her own the one she wishes to remain with."

I can't believe he said that.

"Incaendiel, I have already told you my choice. It's you!"

He looked over at me, and I could feel the pain in his eyes radiate through my body.

"As I said, when the time comes, you will choose the best road to take."

Did he know something I didn't? I wish my memories from when we were together would resurface.

"We were just about to start another memory from the jar. She doesn't have many more left. It seems for every single memory I give to her, another is sucked from the jar automatically."

"How many memories does she have left to receive?"

Lucifer looked over at me with what seemed like a nervous twitch.

"She has six left," Incaendiel replied. "These must be her actual angelic memories. She had her first memory of being mortal."

I sucked in a breath. I looked over at Lucifer, who still had worry written all over his face. Something was wrong; I could feel it. There was something he wasn't telling me, and he didn't want Incaendiel to find out about it.

We walked back into the cave, and I sat down on the blanket with Incaendiel.

He lifted another memory from the jar and asked me, "Are you ready for another one?"

I glanced at Lucifer as he shifted his weight from one foot to another.

"Yes."

He crushed the memory and touched my forehead.

I was in the tower. I sat against the wall crying. I was completely alone, and the pain of the loneliness tore through me. The door popped open, and Lucifer was thrown to the floor. My heart skipped a beat.

"I didn't know what they had done to you. I was afraid they had cast you out."

Lucifer was beaten and bleeding.

"Why did they beat you?!"

I ran to him and touched all the spots bleeding.

"They believe I'm in on the uprising against Father. They tried to beat the information out of me." He grinned wickedly. "They didn't get a thing from these lips."

I helped him walk over to the bed and sat him down.

"It's getting more and more dangerous. I don't know

how much longer there is before they completely catch us in this charade."

I sat down beside him, and his hand touched mine.

"They will not find us out. Our mission will work."

He was always comforting. The room grew silent.

"Tomorrow, I will be sent back again to Earth."

He nodded. We had grown so close together. Will us being together have any effect on my love for Incaendiel? Was this the reason it hadn't worked yet? Was I growing farther away from him and closer to Lucifer? I truly did care for him. It wasn't a connection like I had with Incaendiel, but it was a connection. The silence between us grew and along came an awkward hush to the room.

I found Lucifer's hand on my face, followed by a kiss. During our last moments together, he wanted to show his love for me. Was this so I would choose to return with the others? Why wouldn't I return? The passion between us mounted and mounted. He was on top of me, kissing me all over with my body pulsating against his. He lifted me into his lap and layered my neck in kisses. It was the most intimate moment we had ever shared. There was passion behind our touches, passion behind the kisses. His hands roamed my back to my chest, and I dug my nails into his back.

As we both reached that final moment of bliss, a light burst from between us, knocking us off from one another. It was so bright we had to shield our eyes. When the light disappeared, we both stood and walked slowly back over to the bed. The sounds we heard terrified us both. Lying in the bed, wrapped in a blanket, was a beautiful little boy.

"Damian," I said as I picked him up.

I bolted upright with my vision coming into focus. I looked from Incaendiel to Lucifer, whose eyes dropped to the floor.

"What did you see?" Incaendiel peered at me.

I was breathing hard from fear. I didn't want to tell him. I couldn't tell him. I glanced at Lucifer. The look he had said I had to tell him. Everything in me screamed not to tell Incaendiel.

"I was in the tower." I stopped.

I can't do this. I stood up and ran from the cave. I opened my wings and took off into the sky. I didn't know if either one of them followed me, if they both did, or neither did.

I flew faster and faster. I whipped through the clouds with tears pouring from my eyes. *How could I have done that?* I have a son. I had a son, and he was at the summit. This was why Lucifer was fighting so hard for me. We have a baby together.

I landed on a mountaintop and plopped down. I felt so ashamed and guilty. The last few days didn't amount to what I felt right now. This was the ultimate betrayal. I couldn't tell him. I couldn't, but I knew I had to. There were footsteps behind me. I didn't turn to look to see which one of them it was. I felt like dirt. Actually, I felt lower than dirt.

"What did you see?" Incaendiel asked as he sat down beside me.

"Why did you follow me? You shouldn't have followed me!" I cried.

The guilt and pain surged through me.

"Whatever happened, whatever you two did, I forgive you. It doesn't matter now."

He touched my hand, and I jerked it away.

"It does matter because this I can't take back and just say sorry about it. I can't just look at you and tell you sorry for it."

I didn't even look at him. I just stared into the blackness below the mountain.

"Damian is your son, isn't he?" The question hammered into me. "I heard you murmur the name before you woke up. There was so much love and affection behind it. The kind of love only a mother can show her child."

He swallowed hard.

I broke down. "I'm so sorry." I cried in heaves.

He wrapped his arms around me. It didn't take the guilt from me. I would never be able to forgive myself for this one. *An affair was horrible enough, but a baby? A baby I can't even remember. Where is he? Is he okay? A mother should never forget having a baby.*

"I can see why Lucifer would be protective over you. You two share something that we do not."

I looked up at him as he sat there quietly. I could

tell he was thinking about it.

"No! This does not mean I will choose him over you! It is my choice! No one else's!"

I tried to say it strongly, but it came out in blubbers.

"This isn't even about him or me any longer. It's about your baby. You can't abandon him."

Tears began to trickle from his eyes.

"Do you still love me?" I cried, dropping my head in my hands.

"Nothing can ever stop me from loving you. We will always love each other even if we can't be with each other."

He choked on the last few words.

"No! I will find a way. I will find a way to fix this! I swear! I can't leave you. I don't want to leave you! Don't you understand? When you fell, you took a part of my heart, a part of my light, a part of my soul! I'm not whole without you. That's why it would never work for Alpha. Even if they were to get out of me where the Garden was, even if I remembered that it lay within me, I couldn't give it to them. The only person I can give it to is you!"

The words came out before I could even think them. The words were true. Out of all the memories that had been plucked from my head, deep down, they couldn't find that one. They didn't know the secret my soul had, the secret both of our souls shared. We were created as One, and only as One

241

will the Garden be brought to life.

"How many memories are left in the jar?"

I sniffed back the tears. I had cried so much that nothing else would come out.

"Four."

"Let's get them over with then."

I stood from the edge of the cliff and held my hand out for him. Every emotion ran through me with my gesture to him. A simple gesture, but right now, it meant the most. He looked at my hand and up into my eyes. My heart skipped around in grief. I knew he wasn't going to take it. A wave of anxiety rushed through me. His eyes locked onto mine, and I fought back the newfound tears that wanted to roll down my cheek. He reached out and took my hand.

CHAPTER 17

What is Love?

"IS it better to have loved and lost when both of the loves stand before you? One holds your heart in his hand while the other one holds your soul in his heart. How can you choose between love and destiny, when normally they're hand in hand? How can you choose between those you love, when both are good men...?"

WE ARRIVED BACK at the cave, and Lucifer was sitting beside the river. I was still full of so much shame and guilt that I couldn't even look at him. I walked into the cave, hoping my silence would make him leave. He remained by the edge of the river. I didn't know if he was expecting a showdown between Incaendiel and himself to unfold, but I knew Incaendiel wouldn't hurt him. The only person truly hurting in all this was Incaendiel. A selfless act for his brothers and sisters turned into a situation where he had lost me to another angel.

Right now, I wish Beelzebub had, in fact, killed me at the lake. A selfish note on my part, but this whole love thing sucked and was too much for an eighteen-year-old human to deal with. Even with an angelic soul, it was unbearable for me to think about what I was doing to both of them. Both of them loved me unconditionally. Deep down, I loved both of them as well. The bond Incaendiel shared with me was overpowering, but it didn't change the fact I had surrendered my heart to Lucifer while locked away in the tower. It was an act that resulted in another life form being created, a selfish act that swarmed my heart with betrayal, guilt, and shame.

My human mind pleaded with me. I couldn't

take care of a baby. I didn't know how. I believed my angel self was different, but it was such a big pill to swallow. I just wanted to wither up and die. I didn't deserve to be at the summit. These actions were not angelic actions. I deserved to be in the dark for the rest of my days. Incaendiel would never let that happen, nor Lucifer. I felt that was the only result that would take away the despair I held within.

"You don't deserve anything running through your head."

Incaendiel touched my chin and lifted it to his face.

"Don't ever think about it again. You don't understand what you are wishing for yourself."

I knew he was right, but in a way, I knew otherwise as well. I walked over to the blanket, sat down, and eyed the bottle of memories. Four little balls remained in the jar. Four. I picked the jar up and stared inside it at the memories. If it hadn't been for Alpha, I would already know these things instead of having them thrust down my throat. That is the worst punishment that could have been planned. This was a punishment I, in fact, deserved most of all.

I reached inside the jar and plucked the four balls of light from within it. I stared down at my hand. I glared at the memories. Why they were so important to the entire situation was beyond me. It was my fault everyone was going through what they were right now. Both Lucifer's and Incaendiel's hearts were breaking because of me. They didn't know who I would choose. Lucifer hoped it would be him. The funny thing is, Incaendiel hoped the same thing. I didn't want to leave my other half.

"What are you doing?" Incaendiel asked, sitting down beside me.

I looked at him. I couldn't think what I was going to do, or he would stop me. I crushed the memories in my hand.

"No!" he yelled.

It was too late. The black hole engulfed me, and the last four memories were going to be forced in me whether I wanted them or not.

I sat in a garden that was so enchanting and exhilarating. I had never before seen foliage or trees that grew in the manner that existed here. Incaendiel walked to my side and wrapped his arms around me.

"Father will be displeased if he finds us here in his beautiful haven for life."

I smiled at the thought of being chastised over such an innocent act.

"This place is so wondrous. Mother knows I came here. I asked permission." I looked over at him. "She knows you are here too."

I grinned at him. He planted his lips on mine, and

the garden melted away from around me. I knew I would never feel what I felt in his arms, under his gaze, under his hands. He always touched me in ways that sent me into shock. He captivated my heart and soul.

All the angels had been created with a partner. Samael had Azazel, and I had my Incaendiel. Mother told me we were special. She had mixed us with an extra drop of love that no one would ever comprehend. Forever seemed like a minute to us in our time, and being together forever was always our intention. We could never get past the touches or the kisses. The magnetism that drew us in together was so strong, and the electricity frightened us both. We settled for just holding each other and emanating our love for one another.

Of course, all the other angels had their romances that went farther than just kissing. Some of them had produced creations from their love. We were afraid of what we would create together. We could feel the raw energy that poured through us both. Mother had told me it was the energy of the cosmos. She joked once, saying that we gave her and Father a run for their money. She was always eager to see what we would create.

The timing was never right in our hearts. Whenever we were frenzied together, one of us would always draw back. We were truly afraid of the power we held in each other's arms. Mother told me it was natural, and when we were truly ready, it would pass. I wished we were ready right now. I craved him for more than our passion. He had always pulled back more than me. It was understandable. He had power inside that he held back. I could feel it through our bond. This power had such magnitude, and I could understand his fear of what it could do.

The other angels didn't understand what the worry was about. Samael and Azazel picked at us over our abstinence from one another.

"It is welcomed under the eyes of Mother and Father. Why hold back? You should be embracing it! It feels amazing!"

Azazel had always told me of her and Samael's relations. I envied their romance.

"It's just not the right time. We both have to be ready for the power."

She shook her head and giggled.

"If I didn't know any better, I would think you two are young lovers instead of the age you are."

Angels didn't age the way mortals did. For every 10,000 years, we gained a year. Since we were created by Mother and Father, we skipped a few thousand years of growth. All the angels had expressed their jealousy over us being together. They said Mother had favored us when she created us to be with one another. I never cared what they said. It was Incaendiel who took it to heart. Fighting in the summit was never allowed, but when we were sent to our charges on Earth, they always found a way to nitpick at him. Lucifer had always been the worst. Of course, he had Sophia, but she stepped away from him and decided to roam the Earth in search of herself. It broke his heart, and he took it out on Incaendiel.

I overheard him one day chastising him.

"You can't even be a real man and step up to the plate with her. Always pulling back at the last minute. She deserves an angel worthier of her love than you!"

"You will never understand my sacrifice for her, Brother. Just let me be."

He walked away from Lucifer.

"One day, Incaendiel, she will be taken from your arms. I can't guarantee whose arms she will end up in."

Incaendiel just walked away. He never looked back or retorted to the comment. I found him later at the fountain of bliss. His eyes were always dark until I walked near him. They always lit up like the morning sun.

"There you are, my firefly. I have been looking everywhere for you."

I leaned in and kissed his lips. His eyes fluttered closed like butterfly wings.

"Come, let's take a walk through the garden. Mother granted me permission again."

The garden was always our escape from the other

angels. This is one reason why they say we were their favorites. We were the only ones given the allowance to walk through it. We held each other's hands as we roamed the rolling hills and valleys. There was such sheer beauty here. I knew if we were to ever share a moment like the others, it would be within the Garden of Eden.

I dropped his hand and ran from him, laughing. He always enjoyed the cat and mouse game. I had gained quite a bit of distance between us when I looked back. He was gone. I turned around in time, enough for him to land in front of me, wings open, and for him to close his arms around me.

"Caught you," he whispered into my ear.

"You always cheat!" I giggled.

"You know you love it when I do," he murmured, putting his chin on my forehead.

We stood there embracing. It was moments like these I knew I would never forget. I could never forget the love that radiated between us. Even if my memories were to be erased, I knew that he would be the only one to ever hold my heart in his hand.

"I love you, my firefly."

The garden melted away, and I was staring over the side of the summit. The pain tore through my chest like none other I had ever felt. I stood and watched his wings turn from the lustrous, silvery-white we both shared into dark gray and black. His light began to slowly fade from his body and was replaced by a dull hue like that of the mortals on Earth. My Incaendiel, my firefly, had fallen with the rest because I had asked him to.

It felt like a selfless gesture. I fully intended to help them all come back to the light. The vision I had showed me we would succeed in it. Lucifer walked up beside me and whispered in my ear, "He will never return." I turned to him, and my fury flew through my eyes.

"Don't EVER say that to me again," I hissed at him. "You don't know what I do."

His eyes narrowed at me. I turned away from him and continued to watch Incaendiel descend until I didn't see him any longer.

"Do you care to enlighten me on your affirmation?" he asked.

"How do I know I can trust you?"

My eyes burned into his, daring him to buck at me.

"Because right now, I'm the only person you have."

His words cut me like a knife. He was right. The only other people I could have told had fallen as well.

"What I will tell you is treason. If you get caught up in the plan, you will be punished as well. Do you understand?"

He smiled at me.

"Like you said, IF I get caught."

I fought with myself on the inside on whether I could really trust him or not. I caved and told him everything. He listened to my vision in its entirety, and I explained how Incaendiel fell to make the vision come true.

"If what you say is true, we have much work that needs to be done. We will plan out a strategy and gather as many angels as we can for the cause."

My eyes widened.

"As discreetly as we can, I might add."

I thought everything over.

"Once you have everyone you can find in on it, you have to go to Father and report the treason you have found. You have to turn me over to him."

"He will lock you away in the tower, and then it will never work."

He shook his head against the idea.

"The plan will work. My punishment is going to be what brings our brothers and sisters back home. You must trust me on this."

He sighed and looked at me. The look in his eyes disagreed with everything I was proposing.

"Ok, I will go to him once he returns from the Garden. Mother requested his presence not long ago."

Lucifer's face dissolved from my view, and I was shackled to a wall. There was enough chain for me to scoot close enough to the window to see what was happening outside of the stone walls. Metatron and Lucifer sat talking quietly amongst themselves, occasionally glancing up at me in the tower. They must be talking the plan over between themselves. They stood from their seats, and the door in front of me opened.

"Your first round on Earth is starting. I will be sent along with you to possess the body of your brother. My actions will not be accountable for whatever happens while we are on Earth."

Lucifer stood before me with Metatron at his side.

"Who are we going to be?" I asked, looking between the two of them.

"Father has a raw sense of humor right now. He is sending us to be the sons of Adam and Eve. He hopes sending you as a boy will throw the others off the scent. If they find out, he hopes it will piss Mother off to a boiling point. He said she brought it upon herself."

Lucifer shook his head in disgust.

"When are we leaving the summit?" I asked.

"We will be leaving in a few moments. I thought it best to clue you in on what's going on before you're thrust into the middle of it." Lucifer looked at me. "Are you sure you are ready for this?"

I was silent for a moment.

"Whatever brings them back, whatever I have to do to succeed in that, you have no doubt I will do it."

I had never been so sure in my life. I can't believe

how, over the years, they broke me down, broke my soul down. I was so strong and sure of myself then. Now, I was weak and crumpled. Incaendiel was right, not for himself, but regarding me as well. I couldn't have lasted another thousand years in that tower. They would have completely broken me then.

The chains faded away, but the tower remained. In my arms, I was holding a baby. He was the most beautiful sight I had ever seen. He wrapped his hand around my finger, and my heart broke. Everything I had wanted and craved with Incaendiel lay in my arms, and he didn't get to share it with me. I felt guilty and ashamed of the baby, but it couldn't break my love for the life I had created.

Lucifer had walked to the other side of the room and sat. I had no clue what was running through his mind. I knew he loved me, but he knew that I was to be with Incaendiel in the end. The baby changes everything now. I want my firefly, but how can I just leave this beautiful baby behind? It was a decision I couldn't make, and it needed to be made. I held him and kissed his head. He cooed in my arms, and it brought tears to my eyes.

The tower door swung open, and Metatron walked in with a look of despair written across his face. I knew what he wanted before the words left his mouth.

"No!"

I held the baby away from him. He wasn't going

to take him. He was mine!

"I'm sorry, Sophie. Alpha gave the order."

He walked toward me.

"No, you can't have him! I won't let you take him!" My eyes pleaded with Metatron. "Lucifer, do something!" Lucifer didn't move. He sat facing the same wall he had been staring at for hours.

Metatron advanced forward and gently took the baby from my arms. "I will make sure he stays safe. You have my word. I promise no harm will come to him. My soldiers will assure that."

He looked from me down to the baby.

"What did you name him?"

"Damian," Lucifer answered without removing his eyes from the wall.

Metatron's eyes met mine, with tears falling from them. He turned around and shut the door. I ran to the door and pounded on it. I cried my eyes out.

"Why didn't you do anything!? You just let him take him!"

I was broken and mad.

"You should've known they wouldn't let us keep him in here."

His voice was solemn and mute.

"You could have still stopped him from taking him! You could've fought for our son! Instead, you just sat there and let him tear him from my arms!"

Lucifer flew up from his seat and pinned me to the wall.

"You keep blaming me as if it's my fault. All this is your fault! You and your precious demon! "

"You will never amount to the man that Incaendiel is! You are nowhere near the angel is he is!"

"Well, how about I just take care of him for the rest of us?! How about I just take him completely out of the picture?! Father would be pleased with the notion, and then you can stop acting like such a selfish brat!"

He pounded his fist at the wall beside my head.

"I hate you!" I screamed.

As soon as I uttered the words, everything went black.

CHAPTER 18

Firefly

"I WALK in the shadows craving the light of truth and when dawn emerges, my inner demons shall die and my immortal soul will be lifted into the infinite unknown to start again with wisdom gained from the dark crevices of life unfolded in the pages of flesh and lament. I am a phoenix of the Black dawn and soon I will soar high with wings of rebirth as Ashe dwindles from my enlightened emanation of truth and understanding."

"YOU LET her crush all four of them!"

Lucifer was fuming.

"I didn't know what she was going to do! She didn't think it!"

Like he had any right to talk to me in such a tone. I knelt over her body as she convulsed. Foam ran from her mouth. Blood poured from her nose. Her body finally fell still. Her breathing slowed, and the memories took. I breathed out a breath of relief.

I looked up to Lucifer, whose worried eyes calmed over.

"We need to talk," I said to him.

"Talk about what?"

The guilt written on his face didn't make me feel much better than I did.

"She needs to go with you. She needs to return to the summit before the portal closes."

Lucifer's face dropped.

"Why can't you bring her through the portal?"

"I can't come with you all."

He looked solemnly at me.

"Why can't you return with us, Brother? Are you damning yourself here? None of this was your fault! All that happened was part of a scheme." He bit his lip. "Well, almost everything. You must return with us."

258

"I can't. It's not a choice of mine. It's just what it is." I took a deep breath in. "There is darkness in my heart."

Lucifer slid to the ground against the cave wall in disbelief.

"I am no longer a child of the light. I will always be a starchild. It's not that the darkness won and overtook me. I have always had darkness in my heart. Falling from the light only made it completely overtake my heart. I'm not like the others where it engulfed my soul. I was born with it. However, the light will never return to me like it will everyone else."

I looked over at Sophie lying on the ground.

"I don't have the heart to tell her. I'm waiting until the last minute, and once she goes through, I'm closing the portal."

"There is nothing Mother can do to help?"

Lucifer was grief-stricken. It finally sank in the real sacrifice I gave when I fell.

"No, we have already spoken of it. The light of mine everyone was afraid of the darkness engulfing wasn't my angelic light."

I looked over at Sophie and back at Lucifer.

"It's hers."

His eyes met mine, and he understood what I was telling him.

"You have to promise me that when I give you her hand, you will never hurt her again. You will never let anyone hurt her again, and you make sure she never steps foot back into that tower."

"I thought you said, in the end, it would be her choice."

Lucifer looked over at her. His eyes were full of doubt.

"She would never allow it."

"She must return with you. She will die here. If she is left behind, the darkness will subdue her, but she won't be like me. She will be like the others that the darkness took."

I walked over to him and made him look me in the eyes.

"You two have a family to take care of. There are more important things than me. You must make her see the truth in that. Damian deserves to have his mother. He deserves to have a happy life, not to be caught in the middle of this catastrophe were all in."

"No one will ever understand how you truly are an angel of high authority. I used to be one of those angels. I know I treated you horribly in the summit. Sophie...she opened my eyes to what your true nature is. Even without a rank, you still make decisions based on everyone as a whole. I am honored to have flown with you as your brother. I swear to you, I will never stop searching for a way for you to return to the summit."

I knew it was an impossible task, but I knew what his word meant as well. I nodded at him.

"Well, isn't that touching?" Beelzebub stepped to the entrance of the cave. "Brothers bonding over the whore they share, the whore everyone shared." He snickered.

We both jumped up and stepped in front of Sophie, still unconscious on the ground.

"Aw, such sentiment. Both of you protecting the love of your life, not knowing if she loves either of you back."

Lucifer ran to her side while I stood in front of Beelzebub.

"Remember what I told you earlier?" I asked Lucifer.

He looked at me, puzzled.

"You take her hand; you protect her with your life!"

He nodded. I tackled Beelzebub to the ground. Lucifer scooped Sophie in his arms and darted from the cave. I watched him spread his wings, and he was gone within seconds.

"Letting your wife go with the angel she was sneaking around with; you are a brain teaser."

Beelzebub and I circled each other in the cave.

"I've wanted this showdown since they told me what you did to our brothers at the lake. They call you selfless when you murdered your own blood!"

"It had to be done. They got their strike in."

I narrowed my eyes, glaring at him.

"Yes, but it wasn't successful, for here you are now."

He returned the glare.

"Oh, it was successful, alright. You are just misinformed about the power I share with my mate. It was she who brought me back from the battlefields of death!"

He scowled at me.

"All the more reason to kill her and be done with everything. Screw the Garden! This entire ploy has been nonsense that Father should have realized millenniums ago." He sneered at me. "Since she has been whisked away, I guess your death will have to substitute. I hope you made your peace with her." He lunged at me, and I stepped aside, darting from the cave.

Once I was out in the open, I opened my wings under the power of the moon. Darkness was always my ally. It had always empowered me. I thrust my hands in the air and clenched my fists. Beelzebub ran to me, and I brought my arms down. I bared down with all my might, forcing my power to come to the surface. I was engulfed in flames. She had always called me firefly, her pet name for me. My powers were limited in the summit. I needed the dark to bring my powers to full strength. Once I fell, my powers were uncontrollable. I learned to tame them under Mother's guidance.

When Beelzebub saw the fire surrounding me, he tried to stop in his tracks but slid and landed on his behind. He scrambled backward.

"Your eyes. Your eyes are even flames!"

This was the first time I brought my power to full strength. I was always afraid of it, afraid of the dark consuming me, making me evil. I now fully embraced my true self. I will always be a child of darkness seeking the light. This will always be my true nature. I glared at Beelzebub. The anger that flew through me was replenishing. I remember the fear, the panic, and the agony he had put Sophie through while he forced her memories into her. The terror she had when he stripped her naked and touched what didn't belong to him. How he could do that to a human, whether she had an angelic soul or not, was beyond forgiveness.

The voice I heard next I didn't even recognize as it trailed from my lips.

"You will return to Alpha. You will tell him that you all have failed. They will return to the summit. If he sends more of you, they will die. Anyone who opposes me will die! I am the true Adversary of Alpha. Heed my warning and go!"

He scrambled to his feet and took off into the night sky. The power that surged through me felt freeing. I had been holding it in for so long, afraid that I would never see the light because of it. Well, now, it is written in stone and has been for a while. I will walk through the darkness and embrace it fully. I am not evil. I am not disgraceful. I am a starchild of darkness sent to make everything right again. I am the balance of power needed in the world. I am the Firefly of Immortality.

I turned around as he disappeared from my sight. Behind me stood Samael, Azazel, and Lucifer, with a good bit of distance between us. Samael and Azazel were stricken with fear. It was written all over their faces. Lucifer, however, his eyes weren't filled with fear, but rather it looked like envy. He bowed to me.

"I am at your will, Incaendiel."

I returned the gesture and nodded in compliance. I let my shield of fire drop and released the energy I had held for power. Samael stepped forward tentatively.

"Do you believe he will return?"

I had no answer for him.

"Beelzebub will indeed return, but against his will. You scared the hell out of him just now, but Alpha will make him fight for his side of the cause..."

Lucifer walked to me, and I knew what he was going to say before the words fell from his mouth.

"The war has now started."

CHAPTER 19

*H*ell Hath no Fury like a Promise Broken

"PROMISE...SUCH a word shouldn't exist. A common falsehood of pretentious hope that what is said will be accomplished. Promise...a word that can bring empires to their knees. The easiest thing to do and say, is to promise so happiness will forever stay. But once that promise is noticed, and the words have been broken, the reaction of fury...should've been known to raise hell."

WHEN I CAME TOO, I was back in the Glade. Metatron and Michael stood guard by the door. *Where the hell was Incaendiel and Lucifer? Why was I here and not in the cave?* My head thumped as I sat up from the bed. I expected blood to gush from my nose, but as I wiped away at it and looked, my hand was clean. That was not what surprised me, however. My hands had a shine to them. I raised the sleeve of my shirt, and my whole entire arm was glowing white. My hair was a fiery red and two feet longer than what I usually kept it cut.

"What the hell happened? Why am I glowing? Where are Lucifer and Incaendiel at?" Metatron and Michael stared at me. "Tell me!"

"Beelzebub attacked while you were unconscious. Lucifer showed up here with you, asking us to guard you. He took Samael and Azazel with him back to help Incaendiel."

Michael was the one who responded. His eyes still hadn't moved from my body.

"Have you heard anything from them?"

Terror flew through me. *How did Beelzebub get loose?*

"No, they haven't returned yet."

My eyes darted back and forth between them as I was thinking everything through.

"Should we go see if they are okay?"

My eyes trained on Metatron.

266

"They told us to make sure we didn't leave the Glade, let you leave, or leave you here."

Typical. My mind flashed back to the memories I just received, and I looked at Metatron again.

"Where is Damian, Metatron?"

His face went white. He hadn't expected me to ask about Damian. He had been caught completely off guard by the question.

"You told me you would keep him safe, yet here you are without him. You told me you would ensure the soldiers who followed you would keep him safe, yet they came with you."

His face twitched nervously.

"Where is he?"

I watched him swallow, fighting back the urge to answer. I lost my cool.

"Where is he?!"

"Alpha has him."

My blood boiled, and a fire went through my body.

"You promised me he'd stay safe, and you handed him over to the tyrant who locked me in the tower!"

I walked slowly toward Metatron. His eyes were trained on me and full of fear. I had never seen him frightened before

"He showed up right as I closed the tower door. I had no choice, Sophie. I'm sorry. I'm sorry!"

The rage that coursed through me I had never felt before. It was millions of years of pent-up rage. I knew I was taking it out on the wrong person, but there was no way I could take it out on the one I needed to.

"You betrayed your loyalty to me! I entrusted my son to you!"

Metatron and Michael both stepped back one foot at a time with their hands raised in a calming manner.

"Why should I trust you now?!"

"Sophie, calm down."

The words tore through me like a knife. I whipped around, and Incaendiel stood behind me.

"He gave him to Alpha!" I screamed.

Lucifer stood in the corner wide-eyed. Samael and Azazel stood next to him, glancing at each other.

"I promise you, with every fabric of my being, you will get him back."

Incaendiel walked closer while everyone else kept their distance. *Why were they so afraid? They were all more powerful than me.*

"Take a deep breath and relax."

"How?! How can I relax, right?! Why should I!?" I hissed at him.

I was placing my anger at him, wrong, I know, but he was getting in the way of the perpetrator who deserved punishment.

"You will set fire to the Glade if you don't calm down!"

He advanced another step.

"What are you talking about?!"

He was insane. I couldn't set fire to anything.

"Look down at your hands."

He motioned for me to look.

"I already know they glow!"

I was irate. *How dare he mock my pain at this moment*?

"No, they're on fire."

What? I looked down, and I was filled with shock and dread. Everything I could see that was a part of me radiated flames.

"What?" I breathed out.

Panic shot through me. *How was this possible*?

"Apparently, I'm not the only firebug."

He meant it as a light joke, but it didn't make anything better.

"How...how do I get it to stop!?"

I was panicking. My panic only made the fire grow. I felt like I was going to have an anxiety attack or explode.

"You have to calm down."

He stepped toward me again.

"Stop! I don't want you to get hurt!"

I backed away and watched Metatron and Michael run to the side of the room where the others stood. Incaendiel was now directly between them and me.

"You can't hurt me, Sophie."

He stepped closer again.

"Please, stop! I will hurt you; I know it! Everything I touch turns to shit!"

I stepped back again. This time, he took two large steps and was in front of me. He threw his arms around me, and I could see the fire begin to burn him. He let out a groan of pain, but he didn't turn me loose.

"Incaendiel, stop! It'll kill you!"

He held on to me, the flames burning his skin.

The next thing I knew, we were in the lake. He held me beneath the water as it began to boil slightly. He didn't release me, even as the pain seared through him. Finally, the fire went out, and we burst to the surface of the lake.

"What the hell?!" I screamed.

I was confused and terrified.

"How can I do that? I don't understand!"

He pulled me to the edge of the lake, helping me out. My clothes were soaked from the water, and they felt like they weighed a ton. He collapsed where the lake water met the bank.

"You share the same power I do."

He heaved gasps in and out.

"Is this the power we were both so afraid of? Why we would never..." I trailed off in shock.

He nodded.

"So, what does this mean? What does all this

mean?"

I was absolutely miserable, frightened, angry, and bitter; all the emotions that one would go through at this point hit me. The emotions were overwhelming, and I began to cry again. I had never in my life cried this much in such a brief time span.

"What do we do, Incaendiel? Alpha has Damian...he has my son!"

"We need to find out what he has been doing with him while you have been here on Earth."

Incaendiel sat up and grimaced. His skin was still slightly burned but was rapidly healing.

"Another thing we need to find out is what Lucifer knows about Damian."

I hadn't even thought of that. He just got out of the tower. *Why didn't he demand for our son back? Why didn't he try to take him from Alpha?*

"Oh, also, congratulations."

He smiled at me.

"What in the world are you congratulating me for?"

"You're completely restored to your true self. You are now one hundred percent angel, with your light and all. How does it feel?"

He grinned at me.

"It feels...different. It still feels like it's not my life like I'm watching it at a movie theater."

"It will come together for you in the end."

I sat down beside him, and he draped his arm

around my shoulders, pulling me in closer to him. Even through the sheer exhaustion, I could feel the intense craving my body had for his. The body that truly had waited millions of years to touch him again.

"So... what now?"

He tensed up to my question. He knew what I was asking about. *Sheesh, I can't hide anything from this man.*

"We have to come up with a strategy. Alpha is mobilizing an army of soldiers to keep them from coming through the portal. Once it's open, we have to get mother through and then you."

"No, I want to help."

He stood up and paced.

"Sophie, you can't help! You could get hurt! You must make it through and find Damian. He's more important than this fight."

"Why do you always have to tell me what to do? You need me, Incaendiel. Our power together will take them out."

"I have to make sure everyone gets through that portal. Once everyone receives their light back, they can protect themselves better. This is the only way. That child needs his mother. Do you want him to spend the rest of his days with Alpha!?"

He was right. There was no use in arguing. *He was so stubborn!* He laughed.

"I'm the stubborn one?"

He held his hand out to me to stand.

"Come on, let's go back to the Glade."

I grabbed his hand, and he pulled me up.

"Everyone is going to be mad."

"Trust me. No one is going to be mad. Scared of you, yes, but mad? How can they be?"

Everyone was grouped together when we blinked back to the Glade. Incaendiel made his way to the front, towing me behind him. Everyone parted and stepped back as we passed. Lucifer stood at the front with Metatron, Michael, Sam, and Azazel. Mother stood with them as they talked in hushed tones. They glanced up and were a bit surprised to see us.

"Everything...good now?" Lucifer asked.

Incaendiel nodded.

"Good. We've been discussing what to do."

Lucifer nodded toward Metatron.

"Right, well, this is how everything is going to pan out. Alpha has prepared the warrior angels for this cause for years. They will be waiting at the portal opening for the moment it opens. They're supposed to rush it as soon as it opens, making it impossible for anyone to get through. Once they are through, they are supposed to take out Incaendiel to ensure it closes back and end the whole thing before it begins."

Metatron glanced between the groups of eyes.

"Well, what do you propose we do?" Incaendiel asked.

"We strike at a time they are least expecting," Michael chimed in. "The element of surprise is the only thing that will get as many of us through before they attack."

"And what is the time they are least expecting?" I asked.

"Now," Michael replied. "They expect us to wait until morning to let Sophie's memories sink in or whatever. They don't expect us to open it tonight."

Now, I was nervous. I looked over at Incaendiel as he went deep into thought.

"Are you sure they won't be expecting us right now?"

Incaendiel looked between Metatron and Michael.

"Oh, they are sure," Lucifer replied.

"How do you know?" I asked.

"I've seen both instances out. If we strike now, no one is waiting, but if we wait, they will be prepared."

I breathed in deeply. I didn't know if I was ready or not, but now I didn't have a choice. I felt a hand slip into mine and squeeze it. I didn't have to look to know whose it was. I was awkward to stand in the middle of a group that knew once we left this circle, we were going to go have sex. I felt my cheeks flush just thinking about the word.

Without warning, Incaendiel blinked us to the top of the mountain. It was relieving that there were no awkward good luck or anything like that. In the back of my mind, I was replaying the lake over in my head. I passed out, so I didn't know exactly what Beelzebub had done to my body.

"Are you sure this will work?" I asked.

Incaendiel stepped closer to me. He rubbed his thumb along my cheek while cupping it in his hand.

"What they did to you...what they did will not affect anything. It has nothing to do with virginity or anything like that."

He ran his hand into my hair and pulled me in for a kiss. I pulled away. I was a nervous wreck.

"Sophie, it will be ok. No one is spying on us. We have complete privacy here."

This time, I didn't fight him as he pulled me in closer for that kiss. His lips brushed mine, and it felt like time stopped. Everything went silent around us. There was no wind, no animal noises. He ran his hand up my back while I wrapped my arms around him. He gently removed the shirt I was wearing, and I could feel his hands shake on top of my skin. Electric shocks bounced from him to me as he pulled me in again to kiss.

I began to unbuckle his pants when he pulled away. We had never gotten this far before, and he was just as nervous as me. Without hesitation, I pulled him back to me, kissing his chest. I could feel the shivers running through his body. I finished unzipping his pants, and he removed them. He used his wings to shield himself from my eyes. I realized then that we had never been naked in front of each other before.

He walked to me and grabbed my hips. He began kissing my neck and unzipping the pants I wore. It was me this time that pulled away, but he pulled me right back. He slipped my pants down, kissing my stomach as he pulled them down. He stood upright and lifted me from my feet. His wings moved aside, and he pulled me to his body. I could feel his wings wrapping around my body like a cocoon as he kissed my lips.

I shivered. My naked body was flat against his. I could feel everything, his muscles flexing, everything! He slipped his tongue in my mouth, and I became hot and frenzied. I pulled him to me as if our bodies weren't close enough. He picked me up off of my feet, and I wrapped my legs around him. This was it. This was the moment I had waited millions of years for. I didn't think our bodies could be any closer while moving in unison.

"I love you," I whispered.

The light exploded around us in brilliant colors. I was finally his, and he was finally mine.

CHAPTER 20

Moment Lasts a Lifetime

"I HELD a moment in my hand, the kind that lasts forever. I held that moment tightly so it wouldn't fall away. I held that moment to my heart where forever it would stay. That moment began to falter, that moment began to fall away. But it fell into a heart, where I know it will always remain."

THE POWER from the portal being opened was exhilarating, and it sent a rumble down through the mountain. I opened my eyes, and our bodies lay entangled together on the grass. I looked around and saw the same foliage as I had in my memories when we were in the Garden. I didn't want to stop. The feeling we shared at this moment was so intense. He finally pulled me away from his body and caressed my face. He kissed me, and everything melted away. We rushed, putting our clothes back on so no one would see us nude. Within seconds, everyone was out from within the Glade and flying in the sky. We stood in front of the portal, peering in, but we couldn't see through to the other side. Mother walked up to us, followed by the top in command.

"Is it safe?" she asked.

"We can't see in. We don't know what is waiting for us on the other side."

Incaendiel looked grave.

"I will fly in and see if the coast is clear," Sam said.

Everyone stepped back from the portal as he walked up to it. He was hesitant and nervous. He clenched and unclenched his fists, and beads of sweat rolled down his face. He inhaled his breath and disappeared through the opening.

We waited. Minutes felt like hours while we awaited his return back through the gateway. Everyone was growing antsy after five minutes had passed.

"I'm going in after him," Azazel said.

Just as she was about to step through, Sam came barreling out of the portal, landing on his stomach. He fell limp against the ground. Azazel ran to his side.

"Samael!"

He didn't move. She flipped him over, and he groaned. We all sighed with relief.

"What happened?!" she cried, checking him over.

"They know we're coming," he uttered before he passed back out.

"Everyone! Prepare to be ambushed. They have found out the plan!" Metatron yelled.

The flyers in the sky paired off and swarmed closer around the top of the mountain where the gates to the Garden sat open.

Incaendiel pulled me behind him along with Mother.

"You two stay behind me and stay together."

His orders belted out in a voice I had never heard. He looked to the sky as the moon came from behind the clouds that stretched across the valley.

"Back up!" he barked out.

Everyone moved away from him. Lucifer pulled Mother and me farther away. I heard a menacing groan echo throughout the valley. I watched as Incaendiel bared down and erupted into flames.

No sooner had he brought his power forth than an angel popped through the portal to challenge him. I recognized him immediately, Beelzebub. You could tell by the look on his face that he was forced to be here.

"Beelzebub, I see your father doesn't care about the warning you delivered for me."

Incaendiel had a sadistic smile splattered on his face. It sent a cold chill down my spine.

"I must do what I'm told, Brother." Beelzebub was holding a sword, pointing it at Incaendiel shakily.

"And I must do what's right."

There were no more words. Beelzebub lunged at Incaendiel, who gracefully moved away from the point of the sword. His hands came down hard on the back of Beelzebub. He hit the ground and rolled away to get back on his feet. He flew up into the sky, and Incaendiel took off after him. We watched as we saw a swarm of flies engulf Incaendiel, but they burst into flames as he erupted a fireball from his body. He was at Beelzebub's throat, choking him and then knocked the sword from his hands. It fell to the ground in front of me, and I grabbed it up. The two came careening back down to the ground, with Incaendiel holding him in a chokehold from behind.

When they hit, the mountain trembled from the impact. Incaendiel held him down with his foot and grabbed both wings. He ripped one of his wings from his back as Beelzebub howled in pain. He tore the other wing off, tossed them both down, and motioned for the sword. I walked it over and handed it to him. I stood frozen as I watched him lift the sword into the sky, and just as he was about to plunge it through Beelzebub's back, he blinked away. Incaendiel tossed the sword into the dirt.

The portal erupted with angels. Lightning flashed through the sky. The battle began. Incaendiel took off into the sky with the others following. Lucifer had dragged Samael's body beside us and stood in front of us all as the warriors pelted out balls of light. I closed my eyes and braced for the blows. When I felt nothing, I opened my eyes back up and gasped in surprise. Lucifer had encased us in a shield of light. I didn't even know he could do that. It was impenetrable. Nothing, and no one could enter it. I watched as he fought the angels that stood at the portal. My heart fluttered in panic. There was no one there to help him. I went to leave the shield when Mother grabbed my arm.

"If you get hurt or die, this will have all been in vain."

Her eyes looked through me, deep into me. She must have seen all she needed to see because she let my arm go.

"This is your choice."

I nodded and picked up the sword Incaendiel had dropped to the ground. I left the shield just as one of the angels shoved a sword through Lucifer's leg. Rage erupted through me. I ran toward them, feeding off the rage boiling under my skin, the rage that was placed correctly now. I raised my hand, and a wall fire shot up around them. It distracted them long enough for me to reach Lucifer. As the wall went out, I raised the sword, swiping it through the air. It caught one of them in their midsection, cutting them in half. The other one brought their sword down on me. I raised my hand, and it melted as it hit the flames that surrounded my body. I swung my sword, which was now flaming at the blade and severed their head clean off. Lucifer lay on the ground, holding his leg as he howled in pain. The sword was still jammed through his thigh. I knelt beside him and tried to touch it.

"NO!" he screamed, trying to roll away from

my hand.

"I have to pull it out!"

I tried to reach for it again, and he smacked my hand away.

"Quit acting like a two-year-old!"

This time, I grabbed the sword before he could protest and ripped it from his leg. His scream was louder, and his leg poured blood. I placed my hands on the entry and exit wounds. I brought forth the fire into my hands, searing the wounds to stop the bleeding. I tore a piece of my shirt away and wrapped it around the bleeding hole. He had nearly passed out from the pain.

"How can I protect you if I can't protect myself," he said, stroking my face.

"Well, I guess I will have to protect you this time."

He leaned up and kissed me. I didn't stop him or pull back. I just lingered in the moment, lost. I didn't know what was right or wrong anymore. A part of me wished Incaendiel would fight for me; another part of me knew he wouldn't. I know I felt some form of love for Lucifer, but I desperately needed to be with my other half. I gently pulled away with tears in my eyes, about to tell Lucifer how I felt when we heard a shout from the sky.

"The portal is clear! Go!"

The flying fleet of men who had battled their brothers to make it through the portal rushed the gateway. Azazel and Mother picked Sam up underneath his arms and struggled to get over to the opening. I watched as they walked through with the thousands of others flying in past them. Metatron and Michael swooped down and lifted Lucifer to his feet. They walked him closer and closer to the portal. Incaendiel landed behind me.

"Go!" he shouted at me.

"No, I'm staying with you! I choose you!"

He ran up to me, picked me up in his arms, and kissed me long and hard. I then felt myself put back down on the ground, and a hand grabbed mine.

"Remember what I said, Lucifer!?" he yelled out.

"What?! No! Incaendiel, no, please."

I tried to get loose from the hand that had me, but it had a firm hold.

"I love you, Sophie!" Incaendiel yelled, stepping back as Lucifer dragged me to him, pulling me through the portal.

I struggled and kicked, trying to free his hold on me. We made it through. I looked at Incaendiel and saw the pain in his face for the sacrifice he was giving up.

"I love you, too, my firefly."

The gateway closed, and I watched Incaendiel disappear from my sight.

"No!!"

I dropped to my knees, crying. *Why hadn't he come? Why did he make me go?* I felt Lucifer's arms around me, and I smacked them away. I felt like I was dying on the inside. I heard the moans and groans from everyone around me as they fell to their knees in pain, my pain. Everything crashed around me. My heart ripped in two. I would have stayed with him; he knew that. *Why did he choose for me to go? It was my choice. Mine! It was no one's choice but mine!* I sat there for what seemed like forever, with my head buried in my hands. The angels around me thudded to the ground, screaming from the heartache that tore through their chests. I felt like giving up. I had surrendered my heart to one person, and he didn't make it through the portal.

I heard a whimper and lifted my head. Lying before me on the ground was a beautiful baby boy. He had dark hair and the most beautiful eyes in the world. I picked him up in my arms and buried my face into him, crying. The one thing I had always wanted with Incaendiel was now in my arms and without his father.

"Alpha made off before we could make it to the gates. For now, the summit is ours,"

Metatron said as those around me gathered to listen.

"And what about Damian?" I asked, looking up at him from the boy in my arms, with tears still streaming from my eyes. "Where is he?"

Everyone remained silent.

"He...I'm afraid he took him with him."

Metatron bowed his head. His promise to me years ago was lost in the wind.

"I am sorry, Sophie."

I stood up with my little man in my arms.

"I will search to the ends of the universe for my son."

I looked down at the little boy sleeping in my arms.

"He has a brother that needs him and a mother that needs him."

I looked up to Lucifer.

"A father that needs him to complete his family."

A tear rolled down his face. I assumed that he already knew he had been my second choice, a forced choice.

Mother held her hands out to hold the baby. I gently placed him over into her arms.

"He's so precious. He looks just like him." She smiled down at the baby, and a single tear rolled from her eyes that she quickly wiped away.

Everyone was hurting over him staying, not just me.

"What are you going to call him?"

She looked up at me.

"Xavier."

EPILOGUE

The Darkness Succumbs

"THE DARK finally found a way to creep into my soul. Darkness is all I know; darkness is all I feel. The dark was unbearable, breaking me into pieces. How could I survive in darkness when it felt like I was drowning in an abyss. It was then that I stumbled upon a glint, a hollow reminder of what once was. The glint grew in lumens and that's when I knew, the darkness thrives on the outside, when the light exists within you."

I SAT at the crest of the mountain where the gateway had closed. The hardest thing I could ever have done, I did. I gave her up; I let her go. My entire life and heart I gave up, so she would be happy, so she could have the family she deserved. I knew I would walk the rest of my life on Earth, incomplete and broken. As long as she was happy, I didn't care. Her happiness has always been the goal, the reason to live, and the reason to keep going. Now, she will be happy, and she will be in the summit where she belonged.

I sat there for hours, not moving. I just stared over the edge of the mountain. *If I died, would it still affect her? Would it rip the life from her as it did last time?* I sat there, contemplating if I should just slip from the mountain and fall to my death. Her light and grace were completely restored to her, along with part of mine. I was sure she would be able to survive with half of my grace and light as hers. I teetered on the edge, closing my eyes. Her face was the only thing I saw. It was the only thing that put a smile on my face. Her face began to fade and was replaced by darkness, my darkness. The darkness consumed me the moment I fell. My light would never be able to compete with it. I would never return to the light as the darkness swirled through my heart and soul. I would never see my Sophie again.

My head and heart both agreed for once. I

looked down and closed my eyes. I could never live without her. I had barely made it as long as I had. I was at the point of giving up on her this time. I tipped forward, ready to plunge into the darkness of the valley, when I heard a noise. I opened my eyes and searched for it: a whimpering, a sound of fear and loneliness. The sound tore through my heart. I ran through the Garden that still stood where we had brought it forth, looking for where the sound came from. Behind a rock that sat where the gateway had opened and closed, I knelt. The breath seized in my lungs, and my heart nearly flew from my chest. I reached down and picked up the source of the whimpering.

My heart melted. In my arms, I held the most beautiful sight to ever be seen. Its eyes were so blue that they looked like the sky when the sun was the highest in the sky. The hair was a tuft of fiery, red hair. As I held it close, it latched onto my finger drawing my hand in closer to it. It nuzzled my finger. A tear rolled down my face as I looked into the eyes of a baby, my baby — the baby I had always wanted with Sophie but could never bring myself to have with her. The baby cooed, and I pulled it in closer to my chest and breathed. The baby was so beautiful and looked just like Sophie. *What shall I name it? What was so fitting to name the only light left in my life, the light its mother had left behind for me?* I smiled down at its beautiful face, the face of my daughter.

"Luxina."

SNEAK PEEK AT BOOK 2

The Shining Ones

PROLOGUE: SOPHIE

I SAT ON BENDED KNEE, both in love and with my heart shattering into pieces.

In my arms, I held the light of the world. In my heart, I left the dark half of my soul abandoned and dwindling away. I substituted lust for love and in the end, lust won. I was shameful and broken. I don't know how many ways one's heart can be ripped from their chest and still be able to live, breathe, and function. I sat at the threshold where succumbing to darkness and resisting the light of heaven's gates was imminent. Without my other half, the reason for fighting for all these years, the prophecy seen through my own angelic eyes, I feel like an empty shell. Even with a piece of him sleeping in my arms,

I was filled with hatred and bitterness. I wasn't given a choice. They chose my destiny for me. Along with the tumultuous pain also came a deepened sadness and regret at the loss of my first child. Alpha would pay for his misdeeds.

The sleeping baby stirred in my arms, and my motherly nature instantly kicked in. It was my sole duty to protect this child, this miracle granted to me by the supreme powers that be. He was the only piece I had left of the love I left behind in the darkness of the earthly realm. His name was Xavier, and he was the only light left in the dwindling ashes of the angel I once was. There was a reason I was gifted this bundle of joy and happiness. If anyone wanted to get to him, they would have to go through me.

I grinned through my chagrin at the beautiful eyes that stared up at me. He looked just like his father. His dark hair and crystal blue eyes were nothing but reminders of the man I was tethered to. I cooed as I grasped his tiny finger in my hand and rubbed small circles against the back of his palm. I had been through hellfire and brimstone. I had died and was brought back to life. I was lost, but this gift saved what small part of love I hadn't been stripped of. I had feared I couldn't go on without my love, without my Incaendiel. I had feared that I would lose myself by losing him. I feared I would pine away by losing my son to the hands of Alpha. I had reason to live now.

"Mommy will never leave you," I whispered as I kissed his forehead. "And no one will ever hurt you..."

XAVIER

I HAD OFTEN WATCHED my mother stare off into the dark void of the universe. Her eyes would always seem lifeless, and a single tear would slide down her cheek occasionally. As a younger child, I would often run to her and throw my arms around her to cheer her up. She would always look down at me, and I could see her eyes brighten just a tad. She would return the hug by picking me up and squeezing me and then set me back down where she could return back to her forlorn gaze into space.

Grandmother Lilith was the one who took my hand and showed me the infinite possibilities of who I was. Mother rarely stayed in the Summit. She was quite often with hunting parties looking for my half-brother, Damian. Alpha took him. For what reason, only he knows, but he made sure there was a gap in my family to where we would never be happy together.

Grandmother always told me how special I was. She had never told Alpha, but when she made my parents, she made them different than all the other angels. They both possessed the power over fire, over emotions, and they were both unique. She called them twin flames. I often sat in admiration of the stories she would tell me about my father. He sounded like such a wonderful person and the bravest of all angels. She told me there was something special about me as well, but she couldn't quite put her finger on it, not just yet.

And then my dreams began.

I was three the first time I ever had a dream. Angels don't have dreams, so when I asked Grandmother about it, she laughed it off. It wasn't until I started telling her details about my dreams that she started paying attention to what I was saying. I can still remember my first dream of her...

I awoke in a field. Most would think children would be terrified, but I was not. It was rather strange. I was... calm and at peace. As I sat up from my laying position, I heard a whimper and turned toward where the sound echoed. Just beyond the meadow of flowers was a tree, and a beautiful, shining girl sat there beneath the canopy of leaves crying. She was my age, and her hair was so red, it put cardinals to shame. I walked cautiously to her so as not to frighten her anymore. I stood at the edge of the mound that the tree grew upon and waited for her to acknowledge me there.

She glanced up, wide-eyed and backed away from me quickly, tripping backward. I ran over to her and reached my hand out to her to help her to her feet. She was hesitant at first but smiled taking it. An explosive bright flash illuminated the valley and sent us careening back to the ground. We set up from the ground, and the entire valley had been leveled to dust. She started to cry. I held up a finger and smiled. Grandmother taught me how to grow plants with my powers. She said I was just like my father.

I put my finger to the ground, and it began to glow as green grass spread all around us. The wheatgrass popped back up as well as the wildflowers in the meadows. The only thing that had stood untouched was the willow tree behind us. Everything else I restored back. When I finished, I stood back up and looked at her smiling at me. Neither of us spoke a word to one another. We just stared as if we both were in awe of the other. I held my hand up in the air while she just watched me. Grandmother had been working with me on controlling my fire powers. I lit my hand on fire, and she was startled for a moment. She smiled at me and lifted her hand in the air. She did the same thing, lighting her hand on fire.

We giggled while staring at each other. She placed her hand against mine, and a small light began to shine in between our palms. The flames died down as the light grew *brighter and soon, the entire valley was lit up like the sun. We gaped in awe at the colors that flowed around us. The sparkling lights danced throughout the sky. We locked our eyes and grinned at one another.*

Kasey Hill has lived in Franklin County, VA, for most of her adult life and is a versatile writer known for her work in several genres, including urban fantasy, horror, thriller, paranormal romance, and metaphysical/New Age topics. She has authored both fiction and non-fiction, with a particular interest in Wicca, specializing in Trinitarian Wicca as the historical archivist with an upcoming historical account of the shift from polytheism to monotheism in Abrahamic religions, where she has published non-fiction works exploring the subject.

Her fiction often dives into the supernatural and the macabre, blending mythological elements with modern storytelling. She has published multiple novels, poetry collections, and short stories. Notable works include her *Guardians of Light* series in the mythology fantasy genre, and her poetry that has received recognition for its depth and emotional resonance. As she grows in the horror genre, she has a particular penchant for Southern Gothic storytelling, such as her Adult Horror novel *Devil's Claw* and her Young Adult horror series, *The Whispering Spirits* featuring *The Haunting at Foxwood Village* and *Dark Coven*. She has several Horror short stories circulating for anthologies and Ezines featuring her unique style of worldbuilding.

In addition to her writing, Kasey Hill has also contributed to the Wiccan and occult community through her non-fiction work, making her a multi-faceted author with a broad range of interests and expertise.